SACRED WOUNDS

AN ENCOUNTER WITH JESUS ON
THE HOLY GROUND OF SUFFERING

CATHERINE MULHERN & CRISTINA CONWAY

Copyright © 2023 by Catherine Mulhern & Cristina Conway.
All rights reserved.

No part of this publication may be reproduced, distributed, or transmitted in any form or by any means, including photocopying, recording, or other electronic or mechanical methods, without the prior written permission of the publisher, except as permitted by U.S. copyright law.

Scripture texts in this work are taken from the *New American Bible*, revised edition © 2010, 1991, 1986, 1970 Confraternity of Christian Doctrine, Washington, D.C. and are used by permission of the copyright owner. All Rights Reserved. No part of the New American Bible may be reproduced in any form without permission in writing from the copyright owner.

Layout & design by Mike Fontecchio, Faith & Family Publications.

ISBN: 979-8-218-18893-1

For more information, please visit **CatherineMulhern.com**.

Printed in the United States of America

DEDICATIONS

To my little brother, Patrick.
Thank you for accompanying me.

To my dear mentor and friend, Candida.
Thank you for helping me bloom.

To my best friend and sister, Alyssa.
Thank you for walking through the valley with me.

CONTENTS

Prologue vii

The Valley 1
   Desolate Land 3

Dry Bones 5
   The Barren Fig Tree 7
   The Red-Stained Linen 23
   The Binding Burial Cloths 41
   The Unbreachable Door 59
   The Broken Staff 77
   The Shattered Alabaster 93
   The Unbearable Cross 111
   The Defiled Tomb 135

The Garden 153
   Holy Ground 155

Notes 159
Acknowledgements 165
About the Authors 167

These stories are not meant to be read as a historical resource; rather they are intended to be meditations that are true to the heart of the Gospels and the merciful Heart of Jesus.

"This once-desolate land has become like the garden of Eden."

– *Ezekiel 36:35* –

PROLOGUE

Ezekiel 37

My sandaled feet press into the hard, cracked ground. As I cover my tightly closed eyes with my hands, wishing myself away, a warm breeze dances across my neck reminding me that I'm in a dry, barren land. But I don't need the reminder. My pulsing heart and racing fear won't let me forget.

If I muster the courage to open my eyes again, I know I'll see the same overwhelming scene before me. The same sight that sends a shiver down my spine just thinking of it. The same one that tells every part of my body to run.

Get out of here as quickly as possible! Don't look back, just pretend this place doesn't exist. Run, run!

Leaving seems like the safest option. It would certainly be more comfortable than facing this paralyzing reality. And yet, I know I'll never be satisfied if I run. So I take a deep breath, open my eyes, and look at the scene before me. A deep ravine of desolate land, a valley. A hollow depression of earth filled with dead bones. How vast and dry they are, stacked three-deep in every direction.

The sight hadn't frightened me at first. I'd been intrigued, even curious. *What's the story of these bones? What's their purpose?*

But when The One who invited me here tells me what they are – *whose they are* – I'm overcome with panic. My heart races, my palms sweat. This valley is full of my sins, my fears, my worries, my wounds, my shame, my confusion, my doubts. It's full of my bones, all of which seem incapable of new life.

While some bones cause slight discomfort to look at, others are the type I want to hide away in the dark, dirty, abandoned basement – double-bolted – hoping that no one will ever discover them. *Hoping that no one will ever discover this part of me.*

Feeling all of the shame and fear these decaying bones exude, I want to curl up and never move again. Death seems easier than stepping into this valley with The One who invited me here. I'm afraid He'll leave when He *really* sees me. I'm scared He'll be disgusted, even scandalized, when I show Him what's hidden in the dark.

But there's an unquenchable, gnawing ache within me that can't be hidden among these bones. *I need to walk among this valley with Him. I need to be Known here.*

I need to unlock these doors – I need to show Him these parts of me that I never wanted anyone else to discover. Because only then will I know who I am to Him. Only then can I know how He'll respond to my brokenness, to my truest self. And so I open my eyes and say "yes" to the most terrifying and gracious invitation I've ever received.

I say "yes" to walking among my valley of dry bones with Jesus. This book is that journey.

Together He and I made our way into the valley where we sat among some of the most dreadful, painful, and confusing bones in the canyon of my heart: my wounds from seven and a half years of severe and devastating chronic illness.

Prologue

My enduring sickness of mind and body was a terrifying scene, filled to the brim with bones of pain, confusion, and fear. IV bags, wheelchairs, bed-ridden life. Experimental treatments, out of state doctors, empty bank accounts. Isolation, hopelessness, exhaustion. Loss, desperation, mental breakdown. Not being able to physically stand, and not being able to stand the unutterable suffering to the point that I prayed for death to come. All from the ages of 18 to 25.

I became sick with Chronic Lyme Disease when I was a senior in high school and I had no idea how to process any of it. So I didn't. Instead I shoved it down and endured it all, alone. Years of emotion and hurt dammed up within me, desperately needing to burst forth before the One who Loves me.

This book that my co-author and friend, Cristina, helped me to write is a series of conversations I had with the Lord as we sat among these deeply painful bones of mine. Seven years, seven months, and twenty-four days' worth of bones.

I'd been quiet at first, like most of the characters in these stories. Afraid to speak honestly, wondering if He really wanted to be here with me. But as time went on and I stepped into the shoes of the leper, the bleeding woman, and many other characters, I came to know His tenderness more fully. And the more I came to know Him, the more I could admit and freely express the true emotions of my deeply aching heart.

With the leper, I was crushed by isolation. With the woman at supper, I felt tainted. With Thomas, I was devastated by the trauma God allowed. With the good robber, I felt abandoned. With Mary at the empty tomb, I was gutted. With Lazarus, I resented Him. And with the bleeding woman, I yelled out:

THE VALLEY

"The hand of the LORD came upon me, and he led me out in the spirit of the LORD and set me in the center of the broad valley. It was filled with bones."

– *Ezekiel 37:1* –

DESOLATE LAND

It is all desolate.

The hard, cracked ground looks like a thousand shards of shattered alabaster. My fears, wounds, and sins cover the land in every direction in the form of crushed, brittle bones. Dusty wind blows and I cover my tangled hair with a dirty, matted tunic. Hiding my face in shame from the One who invited me here, I wonder if I ever should've come.

This dry, parched wasteland that expands before me is the mirror image of my groaning heart. The land begs for care and tending. There's such a deep need for healing, for wellsprings of water to burst forth, to soak in, to renew. But the piles of bones are too dry and too vast. I know it's impossible.

My brokenness abounds.

I look to the One who invited me here, desperately searching His eyes for a way out. Silently begging Him to do something, *anything*. Instead of guiding me out of the valley, He leads me deeper into it. As He goes before me in this desert land, I don't know if I can trust Him.

Though the broad valley lies wide open before me, I feel constrained, shackled, bound. My bones have become fetters. Though the terrain is filled with my own memories, wounds, and experiences, I feel like a wanderer in a strange land. Afraid, alone, abandoned. Amidst my own brokenness I feel like I'll remain directionless, forever.

We make our way to the heart of the valley where the remains of a large tree, now lifeless and barren, stand. It seems to have been decaying for many years. The middle of the trunk is rotting away and the upper half has long toppled over, the two beams of wood lay cruciform.

Jesus sits beneath the tree, among my bones, and invites me to join Him. Hesitating, I listen as He speaks.

"Beloved, I desire to unburden you. Will you allow Me to take up these bones from your valley and Breathe upon them, raising them to new life? I will gladly do this for you, over and over again, until your joy is complete."

I take a moment to consider. His invitation is kind, but this will be incredibly painful. I pick up the first bone, turning the smooth edges over in my hands. The wind stirs the red dust around me, blurring my vision. My anxiety rises and my palms begin to sweat, but I know I can't remain the same.

The moment I make my decision I start to feel relief seeping in. I no longer need to carry this burden alone.

I surrender my bones to Him.

DRY BONES

"He made me walk among [the bones] in every direction. So many lay on the surface of the valley! How dry they were!"

– *Ezekiel 37:2* –

THE BARREN FIG TREE

Luke 5:12-13; Luke 13:6-9

"Unclean! Unclean!"

I shout the painful and all-too-familiar words at a group of women who've mistakenly wandered too close. I watch their eyes grow wide with fear and their hands begin to tremble as they register my face, as they realize what they've stumbled upon.

"A leper!"

One screams the identity that clings to my being like a fishhook clings to skin. A single tug causes excruciating pain. I've been called "leper" for so long, I hardly remember my given name. It's been buried along with my body beneath years of open sores, bloated boils, and putrid stenches.

One of the women cries, another screeches as if she's looking at a monster from her nightmares. All three run back to the nearby town they'd wandered just a little too far from.

The looks on their faces are etched into my mind. *This is how others see me.* The worst part is, they're right. I know I've become a terrifying man, if you can even call me that anymore. My face is unrecognizable, disfigured with growths of varying sizes. My nose is severely twisted and my eyebrows have fallen out. My eyes are clouded over, like a dreary overcast day, and my vision has become severely distorted over time.

I haven't been able to watch my body grow disfigured, but I've felt it. The swelling lumps and painful growths, morphing and distorting every part of me with time. Every time I touch my face, I'm startled, remembering what I've become. But it's impossible for me to forget. I watch the looks of wanderers who stray too close to my camp. Their reactions grow only more aghast and fearful with time.

But I know my own disease most painfully, most intimately, because it's the same disfigurement I watched overtake the faces and bodies of those I loved most. My family. Leprosy took each one of them from me. First, my precious baby sister three years ago. After two more years had passed, so did my once-strong father. And only a few months after his death, my beautiful mother was gone too. I was left alone without community, with no sense of belonging. The worst part is, no one else saw, no one else mourned with me. No one even knew of my grave loss. I buried each of my family members, disfigured as they'd become, until it was just me.

My aching hands pull me back to the present from these fresh memories. I don't know which reality is worse. My pain has grown almost constant as my hands and feet continue to become disfigured, bending farther and farther in ways they were never meant to bend. And yet, my mind can't help but wander back to the once beautiful and familiar faces that became anything but their own. I've barely made it over a year without my family. The physical pain is nothing compared to complete isolation, this solitary confinement. I feel like a newborn baby, desperately in need of skin-to-skin contact, left alone in a cold, abandoned place. Crying, begging, yet unanswered. Little

The Barren Fig Tree

time passes before innocent life fails to thrive. I sincerely don't know how I've made it this long without the touch of another human being.

How is it that life can feel so much like death?

The women are long out of sight now. I slowly walk in the direction they came from, hoping to catch a hidden glimpse of someone else. Anybody else. In my sickness I know I'll never be in the company of another human being again, and that realization cuts deep. But I just want to be in the same vicinity as others, unseen. I just want to be close, I just want to feel like a human again.

My eyes burn warm with tears. I want to cry from the depths of my heart, "Someone, anyone, please come close!" But I can't. I'm contagious, and filthy. Unlovable, unapproachable, untouchable. If I yell, it must be that anthem that has become my life's story, "Unclean! Unclean!"

Because I'm a leper, and that'll never change.

In my longing and wandering thoughts I quietly run up behind a familiar fig tree, hiding there. Its rough bark and large, fruitless trunk stand a stone's throw away from the path leading to town. I've hidden behind it before, in hopes that someone will walk by, in hopes to draw closer to another. And when they do, for the briefest of moments, I imagine what kind of friends we could be and what kind of life I could have if I weren't this way. If I were clean.

From behind this dying fig tree they won't see me, but I'll see them. And that's enough. After they pass by I'll return to my isolation, holding tightly to this semblance of encounter. It'll be my solace until, in desperation, I return to this place once again. I know it's a risk every time I come this close because I could be killed if I'm seen. It's only when I'm feeling particularly brave or when the weight of isolation is heavy to the point of almost breaking me that I come. But whether my reasoning for coming here is reckless or grounded, this tree has always been barren. I hide behind it because it reminds me of myself.

A dead man among the living.

A large group of men bound down the nearby hill. One tells a joke that I can't hear from behind the tree and the others laugh. I can't help but smile. For a moment, I feel among them, I feel like I belong. Though I know it'll never happen, I imagine telling them the joke my dad taught me. *I wish it were me who'd made them laugh.* I let myself pretend, just for a moment.

As they draw closer to the tree, I instinctively draw in a deep breath to yell out, "Unclean!" I know I should, but I don't. I don't want to be looked at in disgust anymore. I don't want to see terror in the eyes that look back at me, especially not from these men.

Once they pass by, I'll go back home, just like all of the other times I've come. No, "home" isn't the right word because home implies belonging. I'll go back to whatever you call the camp I've been living in for the past seven years. I'll return clinging to this delightful moment, this brief encounter of laughter with my imaginary friends. They've nearly passed by me, so I begin to step away slowly. A hint of a smile dances across my mouth. This was better than I could've imagined it would be.

Suddenly a sharp crack fills the air. I freeze.

My entire being tenses. My face grows warm and I feel a tingling spread throughout my entire body. I slowly look down to see the broken stick beneath my ever-deteriorating feet. And then I hear the words that I dread most, the ones that I've called out so many times before.

The Barren Fig Tree

"Unclean! Unclean!"

They cut even deeper when they're coming from someone else.

My vision blurs with hot tears as I look into the face of the yelling man. My heart sinks. It's the same man who told the joke. He shouts to the others, "Look at that monster behind the tree. Stay back brothers, it might infect you. Get away, dirty leper!"

I'm a breathing wound, his words are coarse salt. It seems like a thousand pairs of eyes stare at me, all tinged with fear. I look from face to face and wince at the emotions I see. Panic, disgust, terror. One man retches. Shame and a dull ache are all I feel.

My tears fall as I stand before these men. For the first time in my leprosy, I wish my vision was clouded to the point of blindness so I didn't have to watch them take in every disgusting part of me. All of my disfigurements, all of my wounds are on display. Nothing is hidden, I'm fully exposed.

I'm dirty, reeking of sweat and human waste. Nearly naked, I'm completely bare, my skin darkened by layers of dirt. My revolting body is actively deteriorating, covered in oozing sores that fester with flies. I'm no longer hidden. I've been completely exposed without any say, completely stripped of any humanity I may have had left.

Another man heaves, throwing up at the sight of me.

I feel a long-dormant anger rising within me. *What was I thinking coming here? Was I really so naive to believe some imagined interaction would make things better? Did I really think I could experience human connection again? I'm so stupid! Almost as stupid as this useless fig tree.* I kick it as hard as my limp leg will allow.

I'd always loved this tree, so like myself, until today. Today I begin to hate it.

This fig tree is supposed to be strong, life bearing. Its purpose is to produce sweet fruit to tide over the farmers until their work is finished, to provide shelter and protection to creatures in need. *To creatures like me.*

But it's dead. A waste of soil. Just like me.

My anger rages, like a stoked flame. Looking up to the sky, I yell internally. *Why are we even here, this fig tree and me? We're both disfigured, we've been rejected, we're unfairly suffering.* Sympathizing with the fig in an unexpected way, my anger shifts to Someone else. The Gardener. He should be here, tending, cultivating, fertilizing. But He abandoned us.

Though He's forgotten us, I yell at Him internally anyway. *Where are You? Why aren't You here?*

You've allowed this desolation and pain for so many years. What possible good could come of this torture?

You're so twisted and wicked to force this innocent tree to remain for another season. Can't You see it's miserable? Why don't You just do what's best, what everyone is hoping for. Just kill us already!

Just kill me, please...

My heart groans with these questions. These demands. These aching wounds. My tears freely spill as I finally tell this absent Gardener what I've always been too afraid to admit, even to myself.

I wish leprosy had taken me with the rest of my family. I wish I were dead.

The Barren Fig Tree

My anger is gone now, dissipated. It's replaced by a weighted blanket of depression and a steady flow of tears that feel too tiring to produce. I look at these strong men, taking them in. They stand ready to protect each other from me. As it sinks in, my heart is pierced. I'm done. If I lie down, I think I'll die. I hope I do. I lean against the fig tree whispering affectionately, "I'm sorry for what you've been through," and kiss it before lowering myself to the ground.

"Dirty leper," the same man from the crowd snarls, "you'll wish you never came to this place when we're done with you." His words send a panic through my distorted spine. My very breath is a threat. The hatred in his eyes is palpable and I feel terror grow in mine. I clutch the rough bark tightly, cracking open the calloused skin on my trembling hands. Warm blood seeps into its crevices as my stark reality sinks in.

No one is for me. It's just me and this fig tree I cower behind against all of them.

The angry man riles the others. Some join in the threats, yelling in detail the gruesome things they'll do to me. Others bend down, searching the ground for the perfect rock to throw. One man spits at my face and if he'd been any closer, his saliva would've mingled with the sweat that stings my open wounds.

My body screams. *Run! Don't stop until you can't run anymore!*

Attempting to escape on these raw stubs that used to be my feet will be both excruciating and humiliating. But looking at the red-stained bark that I clench, I know I don't have a choice. They'll spill all of my blood if they're given the chance.

Get out of here, now!

I lean into the fig tree one last time, ready to run, when Someone in the crowd catches my eye.

He's ordinary enough in appearance, but there's something different about Him. Coming forward through the crowd, He walks steadily amidst the degrading accusations and the stone-clenched hands. He seems calm, unafraid. *Is He coming closer because He wants to throw the first stone?* No. I can't say why, but I get the sense that He would never hurt me. Something about His gaze is deeply gentle and I feel a momentary sense of peace. I hope He takes notice of me.

When He comes to the front of the crowd He stretches His arms out to His sides. This silent command calms the storm immediately. The mob of angry men falls quiet, rocks can be heard dropping to the ground, I can breathe again.

In the silence, He looks directly at me. He doesn't gasp, He doesn't turn away. I have the sense that He's someone to be revered, but at this moment He chooses to reverence me. I feel grateful to this Man for honoring my humanity. Under His gaze, for a single moment, I even forget that I'm a leper.

But when He takes a step toward me, I remember what I am and I panic. Heat rushes to my face and my eyes dart across my decaying body. In a single moment I see every flaw. Disfigured bumps, open pus-filled sores. They cover me and they smell. *I* almost retch. Even the thick layer of grime that covers me can't hide how disgusting I am.

For so long I've wanted someone to draw near to me, to look at me in this way. But now that He's here, I'm terrified that He'll come closer. *What if He sees me in everything that I am, in everything that I don't want to be, and He rejects me? What if this is my one chance and I mess it up?*

The Barren Fig Tree

I've been hurt so deeply by rejection for all of these years and I don't know if I can handle it again.

He takes another step toward me and I stagger backwards. I'm afraid to let Him come close, but I'm even more afraid that He'll stop coming closer.

The crowd becomes riled again, the waves of the storm quickly growing choppy. A gruff voice from the crowd yells, "Jesus, what're You doing? If that *thing* touches You, You'll be tainted forever. Dirty, stained, irredeemable. Just like him."

Is that pain that tinges Jesus' eyes when the other man degrades me?

"Come on, Jesus, let's get out of here," another one yells. "We'll just pretend we never saw the thing."

The Man they call Jesus doesn't look away from me. Instead, He takes another step toward me. This time I remain in place. He's made His decision and I've made mine.

I hear the men curse under their breath as another yells, "If these are the animals You associate Yourself with, we don't want any part of it." Murmurs of agreement fill the air. The man who told the joke adds, "We'll be in town if You change Your mind, Jesus. But if You come anywhere close to touching that *monster*," he spits in my direction, "You'll regret it, too."

Most of the men turn and sprint toward town, toward safety. Many look back with fear-tinged eyes before disappearing out of sight. Even though they weren't close enough to touch me, I bet they're running to the well to wash themselves just in case.

My eyes come back to Jesus and the small group of men that remain. Realizing how near He is, close enough to touch the tree, my mind suddenly flashes with images of my family. My mom's embrace, my dad ruffling my hair, my baby sister snuggling into my chest. They were the last human beings I thought I'd ever see this close, the last people I'd ever touch. My heart is heavy with this reality.

I stand naked, wounded, completely raw and completely vulnerable before Him. Jesus' closeness makes me both unsettled and surprisingly at ease.

Who is this Man, and can I trust Him?

Jesus slowly reaches out His arm toward me and out of habit I fall to the ground, cowering. I yell at the top of my lungs, "Unclean, Unclean!" Overwhelmed by the pain of yelling this phrase in every human encounter for the past seven years, I weep. At first I hadn't really believed the words I spoke, but after screaming them in accusation over myself for so many years, they soon became my identity.

Laying face down in the dirt I pound the hardened ground in anger, in defeat. My inmost being groans.

"It must be so difficult to live in isolation. How are you doing, My brother?"

His gentle voice and sincere concern feel like a soothing balm to my wounded heart. In my leprosy, I've always made others feel unsafe. No one has ever asked how it has affected me. His words mean everything.

Looking up, I see Jesus on one knee. Genuflecting, He leans down to encounter me on my level. He looks at me sincerely and I can tell He truly desires to hear what I have to say. Sitting up, I share my story with Him. As I lay years of frustration, pain, rejection, and fear before Him, He doesn't rush me. He listens intently.

The Barren Fig Tree

I tell Jesus about my isolation, my bitter grief, the death of my family, the loss of my face and my identity. I tell Him of the physical pain and mental anguish of my leprosy. I tell Him about the rejection I feel every time I have to shout "unclean." I tell Him about the dying, beloved fig tree, the only family I have left. I tell Him that I feel abandoned by everyone who was supposed to take care of me. As I share my wounded heart with Jesus, He receives all of it. With each word I speak, I feel a deepening relief. I didn't know how badly I needed to mourn with another.

When I finish, I look down at my distorted hands, unsure if any of my words even made sense. But when I look back at Jesus, He hasn't turned away. His gaze is Love. I look into His face, really look, and I see the details of another being for the first time since I buried my family. I look at Jesus' laugh lines, His subtle freckles, the brightness in His eyes. All of the corners of His tanned face show hints of joy. The stench of sheep lingers on Him, intermingling with my own scent. With each detail that I notice about Jesus, my anxiety diminishes and I feel more grounded.

I'm so glad He came this close.

I wonder what details He notices about me. My head falls as I think it's probably my open sores and rotten smell. But no, He's already seen those parts of me and He hasn't turned away. Lifting my head again I see Jesus looking at me. It's as if He sees past my leprosy to the core of who I am in all of my needs and fears and desires. He looks through my dying flesh and distorted limbs and He sees me.

"Thank you for sharing your story with Me."

His words are so meaningful to me that He doesn't need to say anything more. But in His generosity, He continues to speak. "You have been through so much, My son. I hear your pain and I know every one of your tears. You are not alone and you never will be. Receive the Love I have in store for you."

A deep smile spreads across my face and a new sort of tears fill my eyes. *I haven't been someone's son for a long time.*

Jesus reaches His hand out to me again, and this time I grasp it. He helps me to my mangled feet and pulls me into a deep embrace. For all these years I thought I'd jump at the touch of another human being, but I instinctively sink in and it feels like home. It feels like I never left. For the first time in my life, even before I became unclean, I feel at rest.

I hear His strong and gentle voice in my ear. "I am so proud of you, My boy. In everything you have been through and in everything that you are, you are stunning to Me and I love you."

I'm completely overwhelmed as Love Himself holds me. He isn't ashamed or scandalized by my filth. He sees me in my deepest wounds and, drawing close, He loves me still. An audacious prayer stirs within my heart and I can't help but speak it aloud.

"Lord, if You wish, You can make me clean."

His embrace deepens as I receive His answer, "It is My great joy to heal you. Be made clean."

Jesus places His hands firmly on my heart and His healing power rushes over me. I feel warmth in the depths of my flesh, my skin and bones pulse with life. Healing seeps into every tendon, every vessel. No part of me is left untouched. In my innermost being, I'm restored.

I can feel my muscles straightening, my hands slowly untwisting. My feet, once-decaying, return in full. I wiggle my toes in their full range of motion and I laugh. I look down at my hands in deep gratitude. They're now strong and smooth, like the trunk of a flourishing fig tree. I run my fingers up and down my newly strengthened arms, which are covered with hair once again. Raising my hands to my face, they're met with unblemished skin.

The Gardener has come and He has restored my soul!

My vision, now fully restored, blurs with tears. I can feel my whole face beaming as I look into the eyes that never stopped gazing at me. His look of Love hasn't changed. He still looks at me the same way He did before my healing. He looks at me as though I was never unclean.

At this moment a new truth is gently planted in my heart, like deep roots slowly sinking into rich soil. *Jesus is for me. There is no condemnation here. There never was and there never will be. He is Love.*

I laugh again, I can't help it! I'm so full of gratitude, so full of joy. Jesus joins in, His laugh is deep and resounding. I look at Him in awe, wondering if my healing is an even greater joy for Him than it is for me.

Jesus puts His arm around my shoulder and says, "I have some friends I want to introduce you to. They will love you."

He calls over the twelve men from the crowd who never left. As the ragtag group makes their way toward us, I'm struck by the drastic diversity among them. Some look like they've come from fishing boats. Another looks much wealthier than the rest, like an officer or a tax collector. Some are fairer skinned, others darker. Two of them even look like they could be brothers. But by the way they tease one another, I can tell they're all family. They belong.

Because they saw me at my worst and remained, I know that I belong among them, too.

One man, built firmly like a rock, introduces himself and the others. We sit under the lifeless fig tree I used to hide behind and they share their stories with me. Each one has his own unique struggles, wounds, and strengths. Each one was personally pursued by Jesus Himself. Their gifts and life stories vary widely, and together they form something stunning and impactful. Each one is needed here.

As they speak, I realized that my personal joys, hurts, fears, and experiences are welcome here. My life is irreplaceable, unrepeatable. In all that I am and in all that I've been through, I'm needed here too.

Suddenly something small drops to the ground at my feet. It makes such a light sound that I probably would've missed it had I not seen it fall. It's dark in appearance, its smooth texture reminds me of my new skin. In curiosity I pick it up.

It's a fig.

I look up to see a patch of green leaves at the top of the fig tree I used to hide behind, the one that I thought was barren. A little blue bird sits among the small groupings of greenery and fruit, chirping a sweet melody. My eyes travel down the branches, which are covered in little sprouts of greens and yellows. When I was nearly blind, I never looked up. I hadn't seen them.

This fig tree that I thought was incapable of producing life is now blooming.

Tears fill my eyes and I see them in the eyes of my new family, too. Without saying anything, without needing to communicate, I can see that the others understand. They pat me on the back, welcoming me in. In the comfort of my new skin, I tell the joke my dad taught me and everyone laughs.

"I am so glad you are here," says Jesus.

"Me too," I say, smiling.

I affectionately pat the beloved tree one last time before popping the fig into my mouth. Heart and taste buds bursting with sweetness, I make my way to town with my new brothers.

THE RED-STAINED LINEN

Mark 5:25-34; John 11:35

Warm sweat drips down my spine. The sun is blazing, but the slightest hint of wind makes a few strands of hair dance across my face, tickling. On any other day I'd push them under my tightly drawn shawl, but today they blow freely.

Red dust hangs in the air, stirred up by the shuffling feet, by the ebbing and flowing of the crowds. I squint through the brightness of midday, unable to fully process my surroundings. I feel as though I'm looking at a framed painting, not immersed in its reality. I feel frozen in time amidst the bustle that surrounds me. The shouting, the sweating, the healing. It's overwhelming.

Looking around I feel raw, deeply emotional. Shock. Awe. Wonder. Hurt.

In my rushing adrenaline even my emotions feel separated from my reality, like they're part of the painting too. Even though I can't quite understand it, I know what's taken place.

The tassel. The touch. The dryness. Everything is different now, everything has changed.

I draw my shawl tighter around my face, turning toward home when a question is asked. It lingers in the air, mingling with the dust.

Despite the roaring crowd, I somehow hear it easily, as if the words were intended for my ears.

"Who touched My tunic?"

The words echo in my mind and my heart begins to pound. *Is He talking about me?* I can feel the quickening beats pulse through my entire body. Skin prickling, face growing warm. My heart throbs in my forehead. I wonder if it's louder than the crowd or if it just seems that way. Even though I'm surrounded by thousands of people I know Who spoke these words.

The simple question comes from Jesus, The Healer.

The massive crowds are pressing heavily upon Him and His disciples and I'm afraid they'll be crushed. There are so many people, so many voices shouting in excitement and pleading to be healed. I cover my ears. The sheer volume is painful. It's so loud that I almost can't hear anything at all.

"What did He say, John?" One of His disciples shouts to another. I'm only a few feet away, but it seems like miles. "He asked who touched His cloak!" John yells back, hands cupped around his mouth. He's lifted and pushed away from the others as he speaks.

The anxious movement of bodies around me thrusts me forward. I have no option but to move with them. So many hands reach out to touch Jesus, more hands than I even knew existed. It's chaos. The disciples look panicked, but Jesus stands calmly amidst the storm.

The woman next to me cries out, "Do you think He can really perform the miracles that people say He can?"

I look from her to Jesus. The healer is wrapped in a pure-white linen tunic that's covered in a beautiful dark red pattern.

Yes, He can.

I hadn't even planned to be here today. I wanted to stay out of the crowd, on the outskirts. I'd planned to observe from a distance, which I've become accustomed to. I'd need to change my linens soon anyway. But with everyone pushing to get close to Jesus, like a mob of famished beggars desperate for bread, somehow I'd been pulled in, pushed to the front, and shoved to the ground at His feet as He passed by. That's when something within me drew me to reach out. Before it was too late, before He was gone.

So I did. I reached out. I touched His tassel. *And now everything has changed.*

The chaotic movement of the crowd suddenly slows and quiet and stillness fill the air. As if there were never any chaos at all, everyone in the crowd stands still, like a field of wildflowers swaying in the breeze.

"Peter, who touched My tunic?" Jesus asks again, looking at the disciple who'd been calling out to John. "I felt the Healing go out from Me."

My heart pounds. Heat rushes to my cheeks, the prickling in my skin returns. I think He's talking about me and I panic. I want to run away to a place where no one else can hear me, and yell at the top of my lungs! I could've done that unnoticed in the rush of the crowd moments ago. But now I can't. Any movement will draw everyone's attention. Now it's the silence that's deafening.

"Teacher, look around," says Peter, gesturing to the crowds, "we're surrounded by thousands of people. Everyone is trying to touch You. You've healed so many."

Yes, I think, *listen to him!* Maybe Jesus wasn't talking about me. The thought brings a momentary relief, but surprisingly saddens me at my core. Maybe Jesus will agree with Peter and move on. Maybe He really doesn't know He healed me. Maybe I really am just another face in the crowd to Him...

"Each healing is personal to Me." Jesus responds gently, yet firmly.

These words feel like a momentary balm to my bleeding heart, followed swiftly by feelings of deep hurt. *I matter to You? Then where were You these past twelve years, Jesus?* My mind stirs with long-unanswered questions, stoking the red-hot coals of anger in my heart.

He repeats the question one last time, looking out toward the crowd as He speaks. "Who is the beloved one that touched My tassel?"

His tassel.

In my heart of hearts I know He's talking about me. There's not a single ounce of doubt in my mind anymore. *His tassel.*

Everyone had been reaching out to touch Him, His flesh. But I'd reached for His tassel. The one on His tunic that reminded me so much of the cloths I've changed daily for so many years. Pure-white linen covered in a dark red pattern.

Please, just leave me alone! I want to yell. But at the same time I know I'd never be content with that. This anger within me – for years like still-standing water in a forgotten cast iron pot – is now starting to boil. I feel the sting of tears in my eyes and I hold my breath, trying not to break into a sob. I feel so angry, so hurt. I want to process the healing that has just occurred, but not here. Not like this.

How is it that I can be so grateful, yet so angry at the same time? Healed, yet still so hurt?

The Red-Stained Linen

Suddenly I hear a still, small voice whisper in my heart, *"Step forward, call out, tell Him what He has done for you."* I know I'll never be satisfied until I do. Heart racing, tears swelling, anger boiling, I cry out into the stark silence. "It was me. I'm the one You healed!"

Everyone turns and stares at me, including Him.

I'd only heard about this Healer two days ago. People told stories around town of His miracles that seemed too good to be true. I didn't pay much attention until the day I saw my neighbor running to the well. He'd been paralyzed since birth.

I'd been leaning against the doorframe of my home, exhausted, when I saw him dance by. I was shocked to see him anywhere other than the mat on the floor of his parents' home, to see him running, to see the abundant joy on his face. Part of me was deeply drawn to the peace he so clearly felt now that he was free. Part of me was jealous that it wasn't me.

I'd grown dangerously hopeful for a moment. *Could this be it? Could this Miracle Worker be the One that finally heals me?* My mind had wondered, even danced at the possibility. After twelve years of excruciating pain, maybe I'd finally experience relief.

Maybe this flow of blood will finally dry up.

But as quickly as the small flame of hope had come, it was snuffed out. My mind quickly protected me from the agony that false hope can produce. Hope is dangerous. Unmet, it leaves a deeper wound than before it came. I wish I didn't know that, but it's an inescapable lesson that comes with twelve years of suffering.

I couldn't even remember what it was like not to bleed.

Part of me didn't even believe that there ever was such a time. I felt as though my body had always ached in its very depths. That the excruciating pain in my abdomen, like shards of glass being dragged across my insides, leaving me paralyzed for days at a time, was simply the reality of my entire life. I'd learned to not hope it away anymore. Hope never stopped the deep, throbbing spasms in my back and hips. It didn't help the exhaustion or the constant nausea. Hope always left me disappointed.

No matter how much I wished it away, the stabbing pangs continued to ebb and flow, day and night, with no real respite. The only semblance of relief came when the throbs slowed to the feeling of needles crawling across my flesh. What others would consider torture was my repose. The pain was fierce, unrelenting. I'd wanted to sob at every moment but I didn't. Crying hurt too much.

The blood had been typical at first, spotting bright red. But it quickly began to grow darker, bringing indescribable pain with it, until it was almost black. Blood that had once trickled, now pooled and flooded, interspersed with thick dark globs. It became uncontrollable, ever flowing. I tried to hide it. I was petrified and deeply ashamed by the thought of anyone finding out. I knew I was dirty, but no one else needed to know of my filth.

The physical pain became matched only by the self-shame. I used seven times as many cloths as other women, and even more when the bleeding was heaviest. Every morning I'd wake up in a mess of blood, which I'd spend hours cleaning. In excruciating pain, I'd slowly gather the sheets to soak them in boiling water. What would take others minutes took me hours because of the exhaustion.

The Red-Stained Linen

For the first couple of weeks I'd tried to scrub clean the once pure-white linens which were now covered in a dark red pattern. But I soon learned they'd need to be thrown into the fire, irredeemably filthy. The deep color of the blood could only be masked by the scorch of blazing flames.

As much as I tried to keep my shame and the bleeding hidden, I couldn't. I was too drained. The constant loss of blood pushed me to extreme exhaustion. The fatigue was so intense that I could barely breathe and I could scarcely hold a train of thought for more than a few seconds.

My secret ended the day I fainted and was found by my neighbors in a pool of black blood. I was exposed. Like someone stripped completely naked before others, covered in a scarlet cloak and mocked. Word soon spread throughout town about who I was.

The bleeding woman.

It was only a short time before everyone knew about my blood, my filth, my shame. Nothing was hidden any longer. And that was just the beginning.

Little by little the ones I called family abandoned me. Some left right away, others tried to stay. But ultimately they couldn't stand to see me in constant pain. And even though they tried to hide it, I knew they were ashamed of me. "What grave sin could she have committed to bring such a curse upon herself?" They'd whispered when they thought I was asleep.

I've asked myself the same question every day since.

And no matter how hard they tried, they couldn't hide their fear that maybe if they got too close, they'd start bleeding too. Those who stayed around the longest claimed they didn't have expectations of me, but they did. And when I couldn't live up to them they eventually left too. That didn't change the fact that I still needed them, but their sense of safety was more important to them than my need. So they'd left.

Everything always left me. Even my own blood.

Then there were the doctors. So many doctors. Each one promising a remedy, a healing, a new hope. And I fell for it. I ended up spending all of my money, my non-existent reserve of energy, and years of my life constantly trying new and painful treatments. And for what? I somehow got worse. And the most devastating part is that I was left even more shattered, even more isolated, even more ashamed than before I'd gone to see them.

They left me desolate, over and over again, until I was left to bleed out, completely alone.

So when I saw the paralyzed man running, I shunned the hope. Because hope is too dangerous. It didn't matter that this supposed Miracle Worker would be coming through my town. After He passed through, I'd still be in pain. I'd still be isolated and dirty. I'd still be hemorrhaging.

This Physician will be just like the rest. He'll leave me disappointed.

So when this Man they call Jesus of Nazareth came to town this morning, I wasn't planning to reach out for Him. I just wanted to walk by, to stay on the outskirts, to observe. Even that was risky. I needed to keep my shawl pulled tightly around my face so that others wouldn't recognize me. If I was seen I'd be driven out of town, or worse.

The Red-Stained Linen

But somehow the mob of hungry beggars pulled me in and I'd easily bled into the crowd.

In the whirlwind of shoving bodies I ended up on the ground, at His feet as He was walking by. That's when the red patterned linen on His back caught my eye. I was taken aback, shocked even, by the tunic He wore. The red design reminded me of the shame of my blood, but against His stark-white tunic it was stunningly beautiful. For a moment I thought my linens could somehow be beautiful, too.

But I'd never dare touch such a Man. I'm dirty and He's pure. That's when I heard the invitation of the still, small voice. *"Touch the tassel of His cloak and you will be healed."* I couldn't touch Him, but I was used to touching linens.

So I'd reached out.

"It was me You healed. The bleeding woman!" I shout out again into the stark silence as if He hadn't heard me the first time. Still holding back tears, I step towards Jesus and do the most terrifying thing imaginable.

I pull back my shawl, unveiling my face.

"I touched Your tunic, You healed me." I say almost in a whisper, suddenly overwhelmed by the vulnerability I feel. I look down at the dry ground beneath my feet. I never knew so many people whispering at once could be so loud. I'm recognized immediately. I hear gasps of surprise and harsh words.

"How could she dare to come so close?"

Head down, looking at the many feet surrounding me, I see everyone instinctively take a step away from me. Everyone but Jesus. His feet don't move. I keep staring at the ground, trying to process what I'm feeling.

Abandonment. Confusion. Humiliation.

Anger.

The coals of bitterness are now hot, licking flames and I can feel the steam rush across my face. It's as if I can hear the sizzle of liquid hitting hot coals as boiling water begins to spill over. Bitter memories of my years of pain and isolation pulse through my mind, tearing through my whole body. I feel the tears start to pool in my eyes as I look up and see His gaze upon me. Is He waiting for me to say something?

I want to scream, I want to shout, I want to yell at the top of my lungs! *I just want to tell You how angry I am!*

But, like always, I shove it down. Instead, I say something sincere, but far from the whole truth. "Jesus, I'm grateful that You healed me. I never thought this could happen." My voice cracks and I quickly clear my throat. If I say too much, I'll break down. I'll cry and I don't know if I'll be able to stop. So I finish quickly and simply. "Thank You."

I look down at the dry ground again, waiting for Him to walk away. That's what always happens. People walk away. I'm surprised that this reality strikes me so deeply, as if my own heart has been pierced open by a spear. My vision blurs with warm tears and I wait.

His feet don't move.

I look up, surprised. His kind face looks back at me as warm tears begin to roll down my cheeks. He looks understanding. "Go ahead, beloved." He says, gently, "You can be honest with Me."

My body screams. To run to safety, to pull my shawl back over my face and pretend this never happened. I could run away and start over and shove this down, too. It seems like the least painful option. But something about His eyes tells me that He meant what He said. I can be real with Him. Not just pretending to be less hurt like I'd done for so many years to make others more comfortable, but sincerely honest.

As soon as I decide not to run – the *very moment* I decide to stay – I begin to sob. My vision blurs, though I can still tell He's looking at me.

"Why?!" I yell.

This question echoes throughout the canyon walls of my aching heart, bouncing off of every memory, every accusation, every pain of the last twelve years. My eyebrows are furrowed, cheeks wet with tears, and I take in a large shaky breath.

"Jesus, why did You allow this? Why did You allow me to bleed for so long? Why didn't You come sooner?"

My back shakes with each breath and I wipe my eyes and cheeks with the full of my hands as the next wave of sobbing hits.

"Why did You allow me to go to so many doctors who belittled me, didn't believe me, and couldn't help me?

"Why did You allow me to suffer the wound of constantly bleeding, constantly feeling dirty, constantly being pushed away from society? Why did You allow me to reach a point where I thought I was utterly unloved and totally useless?"

Each word spoken, each question asked, is like a crack in the dam of my hidden heart. Previously pushed down, contained and controlled, the cracks quickly become gaping holes and more water bursts forth.

"Why did You steal so many good things away from me, stripping me of my very self? Why did You allow such physical and mental agony, constantly? You allowed this cross that broke me, shattered me. You allowed this humiliating scourging for twelve years while I prayed, begged You for death.

"Why Jesus? How could You..." my voice breaks, seeped with pain.

My words and being shake. I sob, speaking between gasping breaths and heaving cries. I don't even know if my words are making sense anymore. Snot and tears flow freely and I use all of my strength to whisper the deepest cry of my heart.

"Jesus, why did You allow this to happen to *me*?"

It is finished. I fall to my knees, weeping into my hands. Twelve years of pain, isolation, and confusion fall to the ground with me. And for the first time since I started bleeding, I allow myself to mourn. My whole being grieves as I think of every good thing that was stripped away from me. Every friend that left, every judgmental stare, every accusation of shame that I came to believe.

Only now do I realize how hurt I was, how hurt I am. These twelve years of hemorrhaging broke me, and I finally give myself permission to acknowledge that.

I don't know how much time passes, but I cry until I feel like my body can't produce any more tears. It somehow feels like hours, and only moments, before my breathing starts to steady. I'm still sad, but I feel lighter. Like a weight has been lifted.

I take a deep breath and open my eyes, looking at the wet ground below me. The red dust mingled with my tears covers the ground and my hands. My face must be dirt-stained too. I can only imagine how disheveled I look.

Suddenly I remember where I am and what has taken place. My heart quickens and my adrenaline begins to rush again. Reflecting on my honesty I wonder. *Was I too brutal, even though it's the truth? I wonder if Jesus wishes He'd never given me permission to speak. Does He regret healing me?* I wipe my eyes and dripping nose with the back of my hand and slowly look toward Him to see His response. What I see takes my breath away.

Jesus is in the dirt next to me, *weeping with me.*

His Divine Face is covered by His human hands and His body heaves with each sob. His tenderness is breathtaking. He cries like He knows the exact weight I've carried, the full extent of the suffering I've endured. He cries like He understands completely, like He personally shoulders the burdens of my devastating cross, too.

Jesus knows my pain and He weeps with me.

As I realize He doesn't rush His mourning, my heart spills over with gratitude and my eyes fill with a new kind of tears. Though I still feel the impact of the past twelve years that left an indelible mark, I also feel deeply at peace.

What a gift it is to be seen, known, and loved by the One who loved me into existence. What a gift that He invites me into His vulnerability and intimate love in this way.

I don't know how long I watch Jesus before His breath begins to steady. When He's finished, He lifts His face and wipes His blurred eyes and running nose with the back of His hands, too. Then He looks at me, *really* looks. We sit together and encounter one another on the sacred ground of our mutual sufferings. He never looks away.

After some time, He speaks. "I know how devastating these twelve years have been for you, My beloved, and I know exactly what they have done to you..." His eyes smile as they wander for a moment, almost as if He's thinking about something stunningly beautiful.

He continues, "I know your suffering personally. Your pain is not diminished in My eyes. My heart breaks at the thought of you suffering. Physically, mentally, spiritually, emotionally. I know it all. More deeply than you can imagine, My friend."

I smile at those last words, finding comfort in being known. But my smile quickly fades. His eyes are sad, understanding. He nods, giving me permission to speak freely once again.

"Jesus, if You understand, then why did You allow this to happen?" He doesn't seem frustrated by my question, He actually looks honored by my sincerity. He looks thoughtful as He answers.

"What I am going to tell you now, you will not understand fully, but you will understand later." He looks off again, smiling more broadly this time as if He can see the whole picture of what's to come, beautifully unfolded.

"I have allowed this suffering and healing to take place because I love you, because I am Love. My little one, I have allowed this because I know the inner workings of your soul and I want to fulfill the deepest longings and desires of your heart. Even though it seems like the opposite, *this is for you.*

"I have healed you so that you can use your hands to heal others in My Name. Your healing was My joy to give, and now it will be a source of tremendous joy for you. You will soon discover the immense fulfillment you find in accompanying others who are hurting, especially those who are on the outskirts of society. The lost, the hurting, the abandoned. Because you know and understand their pain in a way that no one else does, you can meet them in their suffering in a deeply personal way.

"I have healed you so that you can be My hands, My arms wide open. Find the other bleeding hearts. See them, know them, accompany them. Be My Love for them, be My Heartbeat of Love."

I smile deeply, in awe of this invitation that resonates so deeply in my heart. And He still has more to give.

"I make this promise to you. When you are welcomed into My Heavenly Kingdom, you will see all of the paths that your life could have taken. You will see where each path would have led and the difficult and joyous circumstances that you would have experienced had you walked each one.

"You will see that you could have been healed after five years or two years. You could have never bled at all. Yes, your story could have been different. But when you see the entirety of the fruit that will come for you and for thousands of other souls through *this exact suffering and healing*, you will realize this truth. This is the exact path you would have chosen for yourself. This is why I have allowed it all to take place.

"And when this is fully revealed to you, you will overflow with thanksgiving and you will not be able to help but leap and dance before My Father in praise. When you are truly able to comprehend the unfathomable good, the inexplicable peace and the abounding joy that My Father desires to give you through your bleeding and healing, you will not be able to help but sing His praises.

"You cannot comprehend fully now, but you also do not have to wait for Heaven to live in this abundance. I invite you to live in abundance here and now. This is what I have in store for you through this healing.

"It will not always be easy for you. More sufferings will come that you will not understand. But always remember this promise. Your cross, whether understood or not, is never wasted. Your suffering is never wasted. Where there is death, I always bring new life.

"As a reminder of My promises over your life, I want to give you this."

He takes the pure-white tunic, with all of its dark red intricate beauty, and wraps it around me.

"I breathe My breath upon you, My daughter, and give you this commission. Through your wounds, others will find My healing. Redeemed, your sufferings will become a garden bed of life, a source of joy and beauty for you and for so many others. Find the souls who are isolated, the souls who feel misunderstood, those who feel they cannot continue on any longer. Find the souls you understand and invite them into your garden.

"Accompany them in their sufferings, wrap them in the Tunic of My Love. Be My healing balm to others."

He steps forward and pulls me into a deep embrace. I sink into Him. I close my eyes, feeling more myself than I've ever felt in my entire life, even before the bleeding. I hear His strong, steady heartbeat as a new truth sinks in. *I'm healed. I'm loved. I'm wanted here.*

He speaks gently once more, like a father dancing with his daughter on her wedding day. "I have loved you with an everlasting love, My little one, and I will not disappoint you."

I feel a smile burst across my face as I hear the most delightful thing, more delightful than I could've ever imagined. Jesus laughs! His laugh is deep, resounding, joyful. He laughs in pure joy over my healing. And for the first time in years, I laugh too. It's been so long

The Red-Stained Linen

I'd forgotten the sound of it, like the song of a little blue bird gliding through the air in springtime.

My joy has returned, my spirit is lifted. I'm free!

Jesus steps back and cups my face in His hands. I feel like royalty as He delights over me.

"May it be your absolute joy to be My healing balm to others, My beautiful one. Your faith has saved you. Now, go in peace and be cured of your affliction."

He kisses my cheek and smiles broadly before letting out another deep, jubilant laugh that dances through the dusty air. Wrapped in His red-patterned tunic, I watch as He turns and continues walking, the crowd once more pressing upon Him.

THE BINDING BURIAL CLOTHS

John 11:1-44; John 13:4-5; Ezekiel 37:4-14

"Lazarus, arise!"

My eyes flutter open to pitch blackness. Something tightly covers my face. It takes only a moment to realize that my arms and legs are also constrained, bound. *I can't move.* I feel like I'm suffocating. My heart races, my breathing severely shallows, panic abounds. I feel like a pile of lifeless bones, trapped in the inescapable dirt-packed ground.

What's happening? Where am I? Did someone just say my name, or was I only imagining it?

I can't tell if this is a nightmare, but I hope it is. Being this tightly shackled in linen chains would be too overwhelming of a reality. Taking a deep breath to calm myself, I gag at the repulsive smell of rotting flesh. I don't know where I am, but I know for certain that there's a dead man nearby. And by the smell, he's probably been dead for days.

My mind and body pulse with horror and I retch. I need to get out of here, wherever here is. I try to wiggle my fingers and toes, hoping for any semblance of movement and I cry out in pain. I can't move them and yet they ache bone deep. Realizing that I'm trapped in this dark and terrifying place, claustrophobia overtakes every part of me. Through shallowed breaths I try to cry out for help but I can't. Thrashing in the darkness, I look wildly into the nothingness before me.

Cold sweat drips down my covered face, rapid heartbeats pound in my temples, my inmost being trembles. *How am I going to get out of here?*

"Lazarus!"

I know it's Jesus calling my name, and my mind and body still immediately. Though His tone is muffled, as if He's on the other side of an impenetrable wall, I'd recognize His voice anywhere. Even with a barrier between us, I can hear the strength and assurance in Jesus' words. Though I have no idea what's going on, though I'm still terrified, I know Him. He'll come for me. He'll do whatever it takes to release me from these constraints.

I strain to decipher His words as He continues to speak, which causes shooting pains in my neck and arms. I hear other faint voices, too. Are those my sisters? I smile deeply, thinking of those two beautiful souls that I love so much. I don't know why, but I feel a deep sense of missing them, like I haven't seen them in a while.

Did Jesus just say something about rolling a stone? What's He talking about?

The hard surface beneath me begins to tremble in tandem with my imprisoned body. A thunderous rumbling fills the room, like an attacking assailant screaming in my ears. The reverberating sound is so loud I can hardly hear anything at all. I try to pull my arms up and cover my ears in defense, but I can't move. Though my face is covered, I shut my eyes tightly, almost blinded by the piercing fragments of light that burst into the darkness.

The Binding Burial Cloths

All of my senses are overwhelmed and I can't control any of them.

Suddenly, everything around me stills. Soft footsteps approach as fresh air seeps into this place of death. I hear a large number of people a short distance away, their voices are no longer muffled. As I lay still, eyes tightly shut, the footsteps grow closer. "Lazarus..." Jesus' voice is so quiet that only I can hear. Somehow even His whispers carry authority.

"Dry bones, hear My Word!"

Dry bones?

I feel an awakening in my soul as He speaks over me. "Lazarus, My Breath has entered you so that you may come back to life. I will put sinews over you, make new flesh grow over you, cover you with skin, breathe full life back into you. Lazarus, I will do this for you!"

He gently and powerfully pushes His hands into my chest and breathes deeply. A large gust of air bursts into my lungs and I take a deep breath. I feel a sensation of warmth and light flood over my entire body. It dances across my being as muscles fuse together and veins begin to pulse blood and oxygen once again. My chest rises and falls. I wiggle my fingers and toes. This time I'm still met with pain but also slight mobility.

Something has changed. I'm still bound, I'm still in pain, I'm still scared. But it doesn't smell like dead flesh anymore. And then it hits me like a stone slab.

I couldn't move because I was the dead man. I'm wrapped in burial cloths and this is my tomb.

Maybe I should feel grateful to be alive. But my newly beating heart is tinged with hurt and anger. *How could Jesus do this to me? Doesn't*

He know how traumatic this is? And what's worse is that my body is still pulsing with pain, just like the night I died. *What was the point?* Hearing the crowds murmur, I wince. He probably did it for them. He used my pain to draw others to Himself.

Jesus is close. When He speaks I feel His breath. "My brother, take My hand. Let Me lead you to the light."

Though I feel severely betrayed, I allow Him to help me to my feet. I want to get away from here, away from Him. But my face is still covered, my body still tightly bound. Whether I like it or not, I need His help.

My legs feel shaky, the simple movement of walking has become foreign after only a few days of death. Each step is painful, but I'm relieved to feel some of the burial linens loosening with every stumbling movement. Jesus stays close to me, supporting my newly formed body with His. Slowly, we make our way out of the tomb and the light grows brighter.

I know we've stepped outside when I hear the crowds gasp, a thousand mouths begin to whisper all at once. Someone yells, "How do we know it's him?" Others shout in agreement. I'm glad my face is still covered so that no one can see the tear that falls. This is humiliating.

Jesus' hands firmly hold my shoulders, steadying me. I think this is His attempt to provide reassurance. I hear Him breathe in sharply, as if what He's about to do next will be more painful for Him than it will be for me. He grasps the top of the burial cloth that covers my face and slowly removes it. The brightness is blinding. My eyes water immediately and I close them tightly. I can't see the large crowd but I can hear them shouting praises to Jesus. *"He brought a dead man back to life! Jesus can do miracles!"*

The Binding Burial Cloths

Is that all I am to them, a dead man? I feel like a slave at an auction, a commodity to be used, a source of entertainment for others at my own grave expense. As my eyes adjust, my embarrassment grows.

Though I've been resurrected, I don't feel free. *Part of me wishes I were still dead.*

The first thing I see are the burial cloths. Layer upon layer, they bind and wrap and hold my pain-ridden body. Some linen strands have grown loose, practically falling off, while others cling to my sore-covered flesh. I look up from my body to see Jesus watching me. He looks understanding, attuned to my feelings. His Divine Face is painted with dusty streaks of human tears. He puts His hands on my face but I turn my head away.

My eyes fall on my sisters who are running toward us and I smile deeply. Joy and ache mingle on their gentle faces. They hug me tightly and though it causes excruciating pain, I receive their tender embrace. My arms are bound too tightly to hug them back, to hold them. My anger stirs as I imagine what they've been through these past days. I want to cry.

How could Jesus let me die? And why hadn't He been here to hold them when I did? He could've prevented all of this pain.

Suddenly I begin to sob. My tears soak into the burial cloths that cling to me. Their wetness mingles with the scent of the fresh aloes my sisters must've used to prepare my dead body, just days ago. My chest tightens as I realize this probably isn't the first time they've seen me in these death linens. Every part of me mourns. For them, for me.

As my sisters' bodies hold mine, I scan the crowd. Thousands of people are cheering and many are yelling my name. *"Lazarus is alive!"* Immobile, I stand in disbelief. How do they even know who I am? They wouldn't be cheering for me if they knew how much this hurts.

Suddenly the crowds begin to walk away in herds and in a matter of minutes they're gone.

Are they already bored by this miraculous event that has left me so traumatized?

Looking back to the empty tomb that had captivated the crowds just moments ago, I wonder how long I was in there. *How long was I... dead?* A shiver runs down my spine as I think back to the fever and delirium that led to my death. The boils from the crown of my head to the soles of my feet were excruciating. In and out of consciousness I remember seeing my sisters' faces, woven with worry. I'd told them not to worry, not to be afraid because Jesus would come. Oh, how wrong I'd been.

Jesus didn't come. Instead He abandoned me and my sisters when we needed Him most. He was supposed to take care of them. *He was supposed to take care of me.* He'd been my only hope and He let me die.

My sisters' melodious laughter brings me back to the present. Taking them in with my fully recovered vision, I can't help but smile again. They're already talking about serving a great celebration feast in my honor. As Jesus asks them to go to the house and make preparations they beam excitedly. Hugging me once more before running off, they look back as they go as if to make sure I'm still here.

As they disappear over the hill I turn to Jesus. "How could You?" My eyes are warm with tears, eyebrows furrowed. The pain in my tone is palpable.

His eyes show understanding. "Come, take a walk with Me, Lazarus."

I hesitate. *Why would I want to follow You?* I want to yell. But part of me doesn't want Him to leave without me, either. After this morning, I never want to be left alone again.

The Binding Burial Cloths

Avoiding His gaze, I give a quick nod and we walk together in silence. My entire body remains bound, some linens loosely hanging, others clinging tightly to my raw flesh. Every slow movement is painful and I wince with each stride. He walks patiently beside me. He doesn't rush me.

I'm so focused on the next excruciating step that I don't realize where we're going until we're here. The burial garden. It's a private courtyard behind the tombs where the bodies are prepared for burial. The last time I was here I was dead. I close my eyes tightly, afflicted by the imagined scene of my sisters tending to me. Bathing me with their tears, drying them with their mourning shawls. Pressing ointments and herbs into the canyons of my scourged flesh. Wrapping my cold, lifeless corpse in these suffocating linens.

Suddenly I feel more restricted than when I was in the tomb. *Are these bindings tightening around me or am I just imagining it?* My breathing shallows, sweat beads form across my brow. I feel like I'm suffocating. I desperately look around the garden, trying to focus on any detail to steady myself.

The bright, blooming olive tree with long, thin leaves. A hard stone slab for the cold, lifeless corpses. Smooth alabaster jars of varying sizes, probably filled with fresh water and a variety of ointments.

I close my eyes and inhale deeply. The stench of my boils mingles with the freshness of the garden. A little bluebird chirps nearby. As I turn my face upward, the sun warms my cheeks and I feel some of my linens swaying in the breeze. It could actually be quite peaceful here, under different circumstances.

When I open my eyes I see Jesus sitting on the burial slab. His hand rubs gently across the top of the stone, as if He's intimately familiar with it. Part of me wants to hear His attempt at explaining my pain away, but most of me knows that I'll never be satisfied with His answer. How could I be?

There's just too much hurt, too much pain. The devastation of illness, the darkness of death. Jolting awake in the pitch black tomb, unable to move, gasping for air. My heart quickens just thinking about it. I don't care how many people He helped through my resurrection, *He hurt me.*

"I'm so angry at You!" I yell. Jesus looks at me intently with His full attention.

Tears stream down my face and I turn away from Him, facing the olive tree. I watch the little bird hopping through the branches, limb to limb. Freely. In pure frustration I cry out, ripping and tearing at the linens constricting me. The top layer comes off quickly, easily. I throw these death-soiled cloths onto the ground, kicking them out of my way irreverently. From the corner of my eye I see Jesus pick them up and gently lay them on the stone slab.

The deeper layers of fabric cling to me, like a lodged thorn that gnaws on surrounding flesh. But I need to be free and I'll do whatever it takes to make that happen. My hands shake in anticipation of the pain to come as I grab the end of a linen that sticks to the open sores beneath it. I close my eyes tightly, clench my jaw, and pull as hard as I can. Crying out in pain, I look down to see that only an inch of linen has come unstuck, tearing pieces of flesh with it.

Looking down at my body, which is completely covered in these sticky burial cloths, I feel utterly hopeless. I'll never be able to remove them, I'll never be able to fly freely. And even if I could, I don't think I'd survive the pain. I fall to the ground, recognizing that I'll forever

The Binding Burial Cloths

be a slave to these binds of death. Pounding the hard-packed ground of the garden, I weep.

Looking at Jesus through blurred vision I know I don't have to speak for Him to hear the loud cry of my heart. *I need help. I need You.* Without hesitation He rises from the cold slab. Removing His outer tunic, He places it on the burial stone next to the dirty linens and walks to the preparation area. I watch as He ties a clean towel around His waist and picks up a tray. It contains a large basin of clear water and a variety of alabaster jars filled with healing aloes and anointing oils.

As He walks back toward me I consider running, or at least trying to. Away from Him and away from this place. Anticipating the pain to come, it feels safer to escape.

But I'd still be bound.

My mind suddenly flashes back to the day I started following Jesus. We'd been walking back to town after a day of preaching, on our way to the temple festival. We were retelling the stories of the miracles we'd just witnessed when a leper stepped into our path. I'd almost run then, too. But I'll never forget the love with which Jesus looked into the leper's eyes as He embraced him, kissed him, and physically healed him in totality.

Although I don't understand why Jesus is letting this happen to me, I remember who He is. A gentle Healer. I take a deep breath and decide. I will stay and I will let Him come close. The very moment I make my decision, my throat constricts and my heart begins to race again. I'm overwhelmed by a new and terrifying question.

What will He find beneath these binds?

The oozing boils had smelled grotesquely in my last days of life. They're bound to stink even worse after four days of death. I feel them pulsing beneath the linens, screaming for relief. It'll be a putrid, disgusting unveiling and I'm afraid of how He'll respond.

But even more than that, I'm afraid of how *I'll* respond. Allowing Jesus to remove this veil, that both disgusts me and in some fallen way makes me feel safe and unexposed – it's terrifying.

I look into His large, gentle eyes. "I don't know if I can do this."

"I will be with you, Lazarus. I will not leave you."

Standing together beneath the olive tree, I choose to renew my trust in Him. I watch as Jesus removes His sandals and begins. I bite my lip as He pours cool water over my linens, softening the crusty, sticky skin beneath them. My jaw clenches as He slowly peels back the clinging cloths from my shaking hands. Bone-deep pain rips through my body and I cry out in agony!

I look into His eyes, desperately searching for a lifeline to grasp onto. I see my own pain reflected in His eyes, He's my firm foundation. It's as if I can hear what's on His heart without Him having to speak a word.

You are not alone. I Am with you.

Surrounded by fear on all sides, I cling to my Friend with a newfound trust. Jesus continues to tenderly unwrap my fingers and my knuckles. When the pain becomes too intense and I'm about to ask Him to pause for a moment of repose, it's as if He can anticipate my needs before I even ask. He pauses frequently and waits patiently until I'm ready to resume the painful process of being unbound.

Once my hands are free, Jesus places the newly removed linens among the others on the stone slab. Covered in thick puss and strips of flesh, they smell profusely. He doesn't seem to notice. My freshly exposed wounds are sensitive to the open air, aching in a way I've never ached before. I look away from my disgusting hands that shake in pain, unable to bear the rot and decay that came with multiple days in the tomb.

But Jesus doesn't look away. He doesn't grimace. He keeps removing, gently and intentionally. Linen and flesh tearing, cries of pain, relief from the binds, wounds exposed. It seems like this unbearable cycle continues for hours.

After both of my arms are unwrapped, He moves to my feet. Slowly, He pulls away layers of linen that cause great resistance along the way. My flesh oozes, smells, burns. He places each removed linen on the stone slab. The whole time He remains lovingly attuned to my unbinding.

Lastly, He removes the burial cloths that bind my chest. I don't know why, but these hurt the most. As He slowly tugs the cloths away, it feels as if He's taking all of the flesh of my abdomen with them, completely exposing my newly beating heart. When He's finished I feel a deep and grave momentary relief. I take a full breath for the first time in what feels like years.

"Thank You," I say, sincerely. "I hadn't realized until now just how heavy my burdens had been."

Staring at the ground, I'm afraid to look up. Completely raw, completely exposed, I stand naked before Jesus. I'm fully visible to Him, in all of my filth and gashes and stink and puss. I grimace, at both my stench and the pain that reigns in my body. There's so much hidden in these wounds that I've never let anyone else see. But I need to be known by Him in my truest form.

Sacred Wounds

In an act of bravery I look up, and I'm so glad I do. Jesus' gentle brown eyes brim with tears as He takes me in for everything that I am. I see in His face that He understands and cares, intimately. It's as if in a single moment He knows all of the hardship of each of my wounds, fully aware of their stories from beginning to end. He honors them and He honors me. The very act of unveiling my wounds before another has brought a deep healing.

I'm taken aback by the words He speaks next. "Will you allow Me to wash your wounds?"

My wrappings were disgusting enough, but now He's going to touch the very wounds themselves? I stare at my cracked, bleeding flesh. "You don't have to do this," I say. "You don't want to." I know how disgusting I am. I can see it with my own eyes. This Man before me is too pure to be tending to these tainted, festering sores. My staining wounds aren't worthy of anyone's touch, especially not Jesus'.

And yet, in this moment I recognize that having my wounds tended to by Him is a desire that lies deeply rooted in my heart. I never would've dared to ask, but now that He's offered, I can't imagine being loved in any other way.

"My brother," Jesus says kindly. "I know you are afraid, ashamed. I know it feels easier to let these painful wounds fester, to leave them unseen and untended. Please, may I ease this burden for you? Your relief, your deep peace is My great desire.

"Lazarus, it would be My great honor. May I wash your wounds?"

I think back to His embrace of the leper and I desire to be embraced, too.

"Okay," I say, still scared but sure. I give my free and trusting yes.

The Binding Burial Cloths

Jesus kneels before me, bringing His forehead to my undressed feet. He closes His eyes and rests on the holy ground of my wounds. I thought my scourges were repulsive, untouchable. But not to Him. He opens Himself up to their suffocating burdens and takes in the immense pain, the unbearable emotions, and the suppressive suffering that come with every deeply infected sore.

Jesus meets me in my wounds. It's an achingly intimate moment, a sacred encounter.

After a few long, comforting minutes, Jesus raises His forehead. He opens His eyes and softly kisses both of my feet. Looking deeply into my eyes, He speaks with great care. "You are magnificent, Lazarus. Thank you for allowing Me into your wounds. What comes next will be excruciating, but I am here. Be not afraid."

I sit on the stone slab and He gently guides my feet into the basin of clear, still water. Oh, how it stings! I instinctively pull my feet away from Him. But after a moment, I choose to trust and allow Jesus to lead them back into the water. Within moments the coolness feels more soothing than painful. Yet the boils still pulse deep red, warm with infection.

Jesus dips the towel around His waist into a jar of healing ointment, the one for bacteria. When He presses it into the first boil, I cry out. Digging deeply, intentionally, He scoops out the infected flesh. It takes multiple excruciating scrapings. I close my eyes tightly as tears stream forth. *How will I ever survive this?*

I feel something wet touch my feet, probably another healing oil. To my surprise it alleviates the pain completely. I open my eyes and I'm deeply moved by what I see. Jesus is also crying, and as He gently tends to my aching feet, His tears cover my wounds. Jesus begins pressing fresh aloes into the graves of flesh before pouring anointing oil upon them. When He's finished, my feet are free of pain.

In this same way He washes, presses into, and anoints each wound that covers my body. As He tends to my physical wounds, I feel the deeper binds around my soul being loosened, too. It's as if when He unwraps my body, it exposes the true, deeper wounds that lie underneath.

Ever since He breathed life back into me this morning, I've been unable to ignore the internal binds that have suffocated me my whole life. Fear of abandonment. Pressure to provide. The false belief that I have to be perfect to be loved. But through this intimate unbinding in the burial garden, He presses healing balms deeply into the wounds of my soul, too.

And then it hits me. This is why He allowed me to die. I hadn't realized until just now that even before my illness that brought me to the tomb, I'd already been gravely ill in my heart and in desperate need of healing. Left untended, these deeper wounds would've festered eternally. I may not have come to recognize their dire effect without my illness and death. I feel deep gratitude for His provision.

Jesus tends to me for so long, and knowing this, it becomes almost sweet. As the King of kings kneels before me, paying homage to my innermost being, not one boil is left unnoticed, not one sore is left misunderstood. Each part of me is acknowledged, known, and honored.

When Jesus is finished He looks at me and says, "Tell Me what it was like."

As I think back to my terrifying experience in the tomb this morning, I begin to weep. Both of our faces trail with tears as I tell

Him about my death and new life. How I felt like I was abandoning my sisters, how I felt abandoned by Him. How I thought He didn't want me here anymore. I tell Him how terrified I was waking up in the abounding darkness of the tomb, hardly able to breathe. I tell Jesus everything.

"I was so angry with You, and hurt," I speak, honestly. "But this healing has changed everything."

He responds with deep understanding. "Your anger is valid, Lazarus." He places His hand on my shoulder. "I want you to know that even though you could not see Me, I was with you in your dying and in your rising. I will always be with you, My friend.

"It hurts Me deeply to see you suffer, but I allowed this in order to set you free. I know you and I know you feared that you were unlovable in your imperfection. I breathed full life back into your dry bones to show you that I love you, exactly as you are."

I look at my Friend with deep gratitude. In my heart I thank Him, and He knows. He continues, "Your illness did not end in death, but was for the glory of My Father, that He may be revealed to many. Remember the crowds of people that left so quickly after your resurrection?"

I nod, feeling a tinge of hurt. They'd watched, they'd cheered, and they'd grown bored so quickly. The miracle may have led them to believe in God, but it left me feeling used, like a chisel in the hand of a Creator who carves a beautiful marble masterpiece. The Artist is satisfied in the end and the smooth stone is stunning to its observers. But the forgotten chisel experiences blow after blow in making something beautiful for someone else and is destroyed in the process.

"Laz, all of those people who left were following the disciples to the river to be baptized. They came to believe because of *you*, because you were raised from the dead by My Father's Power. Had none of the others been there, I still would have performed this miracle for you alone. But I delight in working with you and through you to bring about My Father's plan. Not only have you been set free, but so have thousands of others today through your story. And this is just the beginning!"

My mouth falls open in awe of Jesus' generosity. A new kind of tears fill my eyes. Looking down at my once-desolate body, I marvel at all of my sores, now fully restored, blessed and filled anew.

I'm no longer bound. I'm healed. I'm free.

Jesus' voice is saturated with sincere gratitude as He speaks. "Thank you, Lazarus, for allowing Me to tend to your wounds. It is My absolute joy." Jesus takes His outer tunic from the stone slab and places it over my head, dressing me for the feast.

Holding my face in His hands, He smiles broadly. "I am so proud of you, My boy."

Jesus pulls me into a deep embrace. Arms unbound, I hug Him back. I can't help but smile. For the first time in as long as I can remember my body and soul don't ache. Like a man healed of leprosy, I abound with joy.

Hearing bells clang in the distance, I know it's my sisters calling us to the feast. The sacrifice has been completed and the meal has been prepared. Seeing the pile of soiled linen cloths on the stone slab, I know I should pick them up, but I hesitate.

"I will gladly carry those for you, brother," Jesus says, picking them up and placing them over His own shoulders. "You do not need to worry about them anymore."

The Binding Burial Cloths

Deep gratitude saturates my heart. Seeing my burial cloths across Jesus' shoulders and now knowing that He brings dead things back to life, I can only imagine the incredible ways He'll use my binds to add to the Father's glory.

I look around the garden one last time. Taking a deep breath, the smell of anointing oil mingles with the freshness of the olive tree. The little bluebird chirps one more time before flying away freely. This place of death has become a place of new life.

Looking forward, we walk toward the feast together.

THE UNBREACHABLE DOOR

John 20:19-29; Matthew 26:36-56, 69-75

My head rests in my hands, pushing my elbows into the rough wooden ledge. My exhausted body pulses with emotion. Anger, hurt, frustration, loss. The overwhelming ache comes in swift waves, like the repetitive motion of a woodworker refining his design. I want to weep, I want to wail. I want to punch these beams, the only thing left holding me upright.

I don't understand... Why would He do this to me?

I roughly jiggle the door handle to make sure it's still locked. I just want to be left alone. *People coming close only causes more hurt.* Turning toward the expanse that can only be seen from this upper deck, my tired eyes drift across the horizon. When they fall on Calvary hill, my vision blurs as I remember how I got here.

Just days ago my life was bursting with joy and laughter. But the supper that took place on the other side of this locked door changed everything. Something about that night felt different from the beginning. The washing of the feet, the breaking of the bread, the Lord's prayer. There was a solemnness to it all, like everything was about to be different. *I just hadn't known how different.*

Judas left early. We walked to the garden. Jesus was in extreme distress.

I close my eyes tightly, hoping I can somehow push away the hauntingly stark image of His agonized face. But I can still smell His sweat and blood. As I push my shaking hands through my tousled hair, I'm reminded of His trembling body, falling to the ground, twisting in anguish. Just like my brother when he fell to his death. *Another brother, gone.*

My body shakes with weeping as I continue to remember. Though the details are hazy, I'll never forget that night. I'd abandoned Jesus in His hour of greatest need, drifting to sleep as He writhed in pain. It was the clanging of armor that jolted me awake, and the rushing adrenaline that had me to my feet within seconds. There were too many soldiers to count. The fear I felt in that moment still clings to every part of my body. Sweat dripping, hearts pulsing, we all looked at one another waiting for whatever would come next. But we never could've imagined.

Judas betrayed our Lord with a kiss that stung us all. I'm still in shock. *Another brother who abandoned me.*

In the chaos of the shouting, we tried to fight back. Peter even injured a man. But we were easily outnumbered. And more than that, we were afraid. So we ran. I don't remember who bolted first, but in a matter of moments we were scattered like wind-blown sawdust. Once a family of brothers, we quickly became a gaggle of fearful orphans running for our lives.

Second to Jesus, I used to trust Peter the most. So when he ran toward the city gates, I followed. Much faster than me, he beat me to the courtyard. I was just around the corner, lungs screaming for air, about to rush to him when I heard his words. They felt like a punch in the gut, knocking the little wind I had left right out of me.

"I already told you all, I don't know Jesus of Nazareth!"

Tears of confusion and hurt had welled in my eyes as I listened to Peter deny Jesus three times, cursing the Name of the One who gave us everything. *Another brother that I can no longer trust.*

Then I started running again, this time away from Peter. I ran back to the garden, hoping Jesus would still be there. Hoping I could make up for my mistake of leaving Him there, which I now regret. But He was gone. The garden, empty. Panic pulsed through my body as I realized I may never see Jesus again. Overwhelmed with a sense of isolation, I've never felt more alone than in that moment, not even on the day of my brother's burial.

I'd fallen to the ground. Clutching myself tightly, gasping for air, cut-covered body stinging from the branches that had torn at my rushing flesh as I'd frantically looked for Jesus. Alone once again, I had my own torment in the garden.

In the darkness, my mind flooded with nightmarish memories. I wish they'd just been dreams because that way I could've woken up from them. But they were real, saturated with pain. The fear, the trauma, and the grief of my brother's sudden death that I'd successfully kept walled in for so many years came rushing upon me with a cruel force. It was like the tragedy of that day was happening all over again.

Climbing the tree together, the branch snapping, his terror-covered face as he fell. My hand reaching out, but not quickly enough. His shaking body, falling to the ground, twisting in anguish. *My brother, dead...*

Writhing in the darkness of the garden, I'd wanted to yell out for help. I'd wanted to cry out for Jesus to come! But I knew it was in vain. What did it matter anyway? He was as good as dead, too.

I don't know how I survived the mental anguish of that night, but I wish I hadn't. I'd thought coming back to this upper room, back to my brother disciples, would somehow help. But when I got here it was empty, untouched. There were still cups on the table and Judas' chalice lay sprawled on the ground where it had fallen. The money bag had hit it when he'd quickly left supper. *Oh, Judas...* My heart aches for him, for me. *Is there anyone I can trust?*

I'd run out onto this upper deck when I heard the yelling crowds. Their accusations were louder than usual and blood-curdling screams could be heard from every direction. I knew there was probably a crucifixion taking place, I just didn't know who the criminal was this time.

But when I heard the crowds yelling His Name, cursing Him like Peter had, I realized what was happening. I fell to my knees and wailed. From this very deck I saw Jesus cry out in pain. I heard the pounding of hammers hitting nails, metal tearing flesh, iron crushing bone. I watched the unthinkable occur.

I lost another Brother to death by a tree.

I didn't want to watch, but I also couldn't look away. Through warm, blurred vision, I felt the grief like a spear piercing my own side. It was so ravishing I could hardly feel it at all. I'm still numb.

As the following hazy hours unfolded, the others made their way back to the upper room. I thought it would be helpful to come together, to no longer be alone. But I soon realized I couldn't handle the tears and grief, the hurt and confusion of the others in addition to my own. My sorrow was already too much to bear.

So I'd taken food and a blanket and I came back to this upper deck, the only place left that I feel some semblance of safety, locking the door behind me.

The Unbreachable Door

I've been here ever since.

Calvary hill looks different now, days later. The crosses are gone, the crowds dispersed, the criminals dead. And although a peaceful silence fills the air, death and torment are still all I see on that dirt-packed mound. They're all I'll ever see.

As a cool breeze dances across my damp cheeks, my grip tightens on the railing. Splinters from the rough wood split my skin, and my fingers scream in pain. But I don't care. I scarcely resist the urge to yell and for a moment I consider climbing over the railing to end it all, falling to the same death as my brother. But I'm too tired to lift my exhausted body and soul, which are severely weighed down by layers of grief.

My tired eyes wander, looking away from Calvary – to anything but that desolate hill. My gaze falls upon my childhood home. I can just see the roofline from here, weathered from years of sheltering my now dispersed family. I wince, seeing that tall tree, still swaying gently in the wind, as if nothing life-altering had happened there. I haven't looked at it in a long time, I haven't been able to. And now, in some twisted way, it's all I have left.

Though the tree is somewhat near, the innocence I once experienced there feels miles away. I smile slightly as I remember how our mother used to yell at us for sitting high up in its branches. I'd climb on my twin brother's shoulders anyway, pulling him up after me. We spent hours there, swaying with the wind, feeling like we were on top of the world. Watching the neighborhood children try to catch chickens, throwing fruit at unsuspecting travelers passing through, gazing at the stars and dreaming of the adventures to come.

We were best friends, inseparable. At least we'd thought so.

We'd been laughing, scheming about switching places and tricking our old neighbor again. That's when the branch snapped beneath him, breaking my world apart with it. I can still hear the sound distinctly, followed by my scream in tandem with his. Crying out in fear was the last thing we did together. When his body hit the ground, it sounded eerily similar to the breaking branch. He simply crumpled and then he was gone. For a long time I stayed there, hand extended, met only with emptiness.

I pull my gaze away from the tree, anger boiling within me. If I ever leave this deck I'll cut that tree down, taking its life breath like it took my brother's. But the emotion within me quickly subsides, giving way to an overwhelming wave of fatigue. I feel defeated.

The sunlight gleams along the dome of the synagogue, drawing my heavy eyes to the place I first met Jesus. That day had been especially difficult for me. It had been fifteen years since my brother's death and we'd gone to mourn his loss once again. I stood on the familiar dirt-packed earth, now hard and dry, and stared at the gravestone of my twin brother.

The window shutters of the synagogue were open, and as a cool breeze drifted in, the calming voice of Jesus' preaching seeped out. I still remember His words that struck a chord within me. He spoke about a new kind of family, one that was eternal. I remember the anger that I'd felt. *If He was capable of such things then why hadn't He kept my family together?* I'm still wondering...

I remember kneeling before my brother's burial plot, weeping. Placing my hand on the ground that covered his now-decayed body. I wish he were still here to be angry with me. When I felt a hand on my shoulder, I turned, expecting to see my father. Instead, I saw Jesus.

His dark eyes, which reminded me so much of my brother's, were filled with deep kindness. He reached out His hand to me and said something I'll never forget.

"Come, follow Me, brother."

I hadn't been someone's brother in a long time, and I was deeply moved. But as I imagined reaching out my hand toward Him, all I could see was my twin falling. I was terrified that my hand would be met with emptiness once again. And yet, there was something different about this Man, something drawing about this unique call He spoke over me. I suddenly felt a deep sense of peace and a desire to be part of this family He spoke of.

I never thought I'd be able to trust someone again, in fear that they'd be torn away from me, too. For fifteen years I'd built a wall of protection around my heart, and in that moment, Jesus removed the first brick. And I could feel the freedom that came with its removal.

So I said yes. I'd lifted my hand from my brother's tomb and grasped onto His.

Now I realize it was the greatest mistake I've ever made. That day I hadn't known that I was saying yes to another grave loss, another Brother abandoning me.

The three years that followed that day at the synagogue were some of the best in my life. It was an incredible adventure. I gained twelve new brothers and we became like the family Jesus had preached about. We ministered together and witnessed magnificent miracles we never could have dreamed possible. We battled storms on raging seas and swam in the Sea of Galilee after long hours of fishing. We prayed and broke bread together, we supported one another.

Each experience felt like a healing balm to the wound of losing my brother. A restoration of sorts. With each small healing, each smile and deep laugh that brought me back to life, I felt Jesus continuing to take down the wall that once protected my heart, brick-by-brick.

It feels almost laughable now. I feel tricked, like Jesus was knocking down my wall just to hurt me all over again. Tears welling, I yell out into the empty view in front of me.

"Where are You now?!"

I reach my arm out over the ledge of the deck and it's met with emptiness once again.

He'd promised this would never happen and look where that got me. You know what almost hurts more than losing my brother? Having been gifted a new community, becoming so attached, so engrained only to have that torn away, too.

How could Jesus do this to me, especially knowing of my grave loss?

If I'd known this is what following Him would get me, I never would've grasped His hand that day at the synagogue. I would've stayed with my brother, mourning until I was buried, too.

Suddenly I hear shouting in the upper room where the other disciples have been staying. *Are they celebrating? They sound... happy.* I unlock the door and run through it, shocked by the sight I see. The room is full of this group I once called my community, each man is beaming, many are leaping joyfully, some are even dancing.

"What happened?" I shout, trying to hide the pain in my voice.

The Unbreachable Door

Their responses come so loudly and in unison that I can hardly hear any of them at all. "We just saw Jesus, He came right through the locked doors!" "He's risen!" "He's alive!"

Their words are like a punch in the gut. After all of my trauma, all of my loss, *He appeared to everyone but me.*

Overwhelmed with devastation I run back to the balcony, slamming the door behind me. As I lock it once again, I rebuild in an instant the wall around my heart that Jesus had spent so many years taking down. If I had brick and mortar, I would physically board up this door between me and the others, making it unbreachable. I never want to be vulnerable again, it's easier to just stay away from everyone.

I hear banging on the door and shouting from inside. Their voices drip with pity and it stings. Even they realize what's taken place.

"Please, Thomas, come back inside!" "We saw the scars on His hands and feet!" "*Our Brother is alive!*"

These last words make me go cold. Jesus is not my Brother. I don't want to believe them that He's alive again, but I know it's true. We'd seen Him bring dead things back to life before. *But why would He appear without me there? Doesn't He know how much this hurts?*

This betrayal is the gravest loss I've ever experienced. In deep pain manifested as rage, I slam my fists against the door, yelling back, "Unless I put my fingers in the nail marks and put my hand in His side, I will not believe!"

I shout these words in disrespect, as if pushing my fingers deeply into His open wounds like He has pushed into mine. The audacity and disrespect that come from my mouth surprise even me, but I mean every word. I hear the others gasp, and though their voices are distorted through the thickness of the door, I couldn't have heard them more clearly.

"I'm not surprised. Thomas has always doubted, anyway."

I run to the edge of the deck, thinking of jumping again. What hurts most is that they're right.

As cold tears run down my cheeks, my heart is hardened. Once more checking the lock on the door between me and the others, I take the key and throw it off the deck. I hear it hit the hard ground somewhere far below. I hope it shattered. Though part of me wishes someone would fight to break the door down and convince me to come back inside, I know they won't. I've pushed them all away. *I wouldn't want to be with me, either.*

Lifting my leg over the handrail, ready to jump, I hear soft footsteps approaching. I know Who it is immediately. As my emotions swell within me, I don't know whether to lean into Him or into the abyss below.

How can I ever trust this Man again?

"Thomas." His voice is sturdy, gentle.

I wonder if I'm just imagining it all in my exhaustion, like a tormented illusion my mind has created. But when I feel a hand on my shoulder, I turn and see that it's really Jesus. He looks so Himself, yet different. So human, yet glorified. Without even meaning to, I begin to lean toward the fall. But He catches me, drawing me into Himself and I weep.

I'm so overwhelmed. By fear, hurt, confusion. A deep ache has taken up permanent residence in my heart. And I feel something new rush over me. Guilt. *I doubted when I should've believed.* And worse yet, even though He's standing before me, I still have more doubts.

Jesus says no words, He asks no questions. He simply allows me to feel as waves of grief flood over me. The death of my brother. My betrayal of Jesus, my cowardice. My own torment in the garden. The chaos of that night, how I'd almost just jumped.

All the loss, all the pain, all the hurt.

Why is He even here?

My face grows warm, my heart pulses in panic. Maybe He's here to tell me I no longer belong to His family. Maybe that's why He appeared to everyone but me. I've doubted Him, I've denied Him. I wouldn't blame Him if He doesn't want me anymore. Maybe He's going to–

"Thomas."

My internal accusations cease at the sound of His voice. He continues, "I came to meet you here because I know this is where you feel safest."

Though my body is still saturated with anger and hurt, I feel seen and understood in a way that I can't even understand myself. He's right, I don't feel safe around the others, I don't feel safe anywhere else. For the first time since I stepped out onto this deck, I look past my emotions that are steeped in guilt and I look upon myself with the same gentleness that He does.

I'm hurt and I need to feel safe.

Looking across the deck my eyes catch sight of Calvary hill again, the place that destroyed everything. In an instant my body floods with panic. As quickly as He returned, He could leave me again. *What will I do if Jesus leaves me again?*

"Thomas."

The way He says my name is grounding. I look toward Him and gasp. He's pulling back His tunic, slowly unveiling His wounds to me. His torn flesh is somehow glorious. I immediately take a step back, fully aware of my unworthiness. The words I'd just yelled through the door echo in my ears.

Unless I touch, unless I push into His wounds, I will not believe.

I'm so glad He didn't hear me say these words. They probably would've stung more than Judas' kiss.

How am I supposed to express to Him that I was so hurt that I wanted to hurt Him back? That I'd disrespected His sacrifice? He definitely won't want me anymore after He finds out. Overcome with shame, I want to run away but there's nowhere to go. In vain I frantically search this tiny balcony, but there's no place to hide.

Everything in my body is telling me to build walls, to lock doors like I always have. As I desperately look in all directions, the tree swaying next to my childhood home catches my eye again. *I bet my brother would be ashamed of me, too.*

Jesus steps closer.

"No!" I yell, throwing up my hands. "You don't know me, I'm not worthy!"

Taking another step toward me, Jesus keeps His eyes on mine. "Brother, I do know you. I know your story. I know the weight of your sorrows and the burdens you bear." My tears spill over, sobs heave in my chest as He continues. "I know that seeing My death brought all of your trauma up again. I know how devastated, how hurt, how afraid you are. I know you are not okay, Thomas, and that is okay."

"Then why'd You let it happen?" The edges of my mouth quiver, my voice breaks. "Why did You appear to everyone but me?"

The other disciples hadn't known about my pain, my past traumas. But Jesus knew, and He did this anyway. Jesus pauses thoughtfully, as if taking a moment to pay respect to my true and deep emotions.

When He responds, His tone is kind. "Because I know you."

"I knew My death would affect you in a deeper way than the others. You have experienced devastating personal loss, unlike many of your brothers. You have a deeply sensitive heart. I did not appear to you with the others because I knew you needed to experience this on your own. I knew you needed this moment between us, just Me and you. I am appearing to you on this upper deck so that you have the opportunity to speak your heart freely. What you have to say matters to Me."

His words are like a key in the deadbolt lock of my heart. I hope He enters in.

But He still doesn't know what I said about His wounds. If He knew, He'd probably throw the key off the deck's ledge, too. As if understanding my tormented thoughts, Jesus holds out His scarred hands toward me.

"Thomas, I am appearing to you in intimacy so that I can show you this part of Me."

I never knew human flesh could be so stunning. For a moment I wonder if His skin is illuminating. His eyes look eager, even excited, like He's long awaited to give me this gift. But I don't deserve to receive it. I look away from His gaze, enveloped in my shame.

"I am appearing to you here so that you can touch My wounds."

His words shock me and the hair on my neck stands straight up. *If only He knew...* With eyes turned downward, I shake my head. My voice trembles. "You don't understand, Jesus. You don't know what I said. I–"

"I know what you said, Thomas." No judgment can be heard anywhere in His voice. "But I also know your words were spoken out of a place of deep hurt, not out of hate. Your words were a cry of your broken, locked up heart. In frustration you demanded something that seemed impossible. In love, I want to fulfill that desire for you."

Gaze still on the ground, I speak in true contrition. "I'm sorry, Jesus. Please help my unbelief."

"I forgive you, My boy." He speaks without hesitation and His words are like a breath of fresh air, a permission I didn't know I'd so deeply been longing for. "I know you, My Thomas. In order to believe, you need to touch, you need to see, you need to *feel*. This is not a weakness. This is how My Father created you, and I love this about you!"

I'm so moved I can hardly breathe. Who am I to receive such a love as this? Who am I that Jesus should not only care to enter into my heart, but that He's willing to make His way through the bolt-locked door. All to tend to me.

Looking up, I see His hands extended toward me. Reaching forward in fear and awe, I place my fingers within His wounds. As our flesh touches, I feel an electric pulse echo throughout my entire body. It's as if I can *feel* His light spreading within every part of me. A surge of peace accompanies the light and I feel like His wounds are somehow transfiguring me.

Though I can't grasp the magnitude of it all, I know there's glory in these wounds. Once a sign of torture, now a means of healing. Once a tell of death, now a source of life.

As the light spreads throughout my being, it seems to touch every one of my wounds, every memory with restoration. Even the death of my twin brother – my gravest loss – is sanctified. A wave of peace crashes over me and I know that somehow, through Jesus' glorified wounds, my brother has been healed, too. Without a doubt I feel that one day we'll be together again. I still miss my brother dearly, but the seemingly irredeemable ache of his death has lost its sting.

I know in my heart that Jesus died *for me*. The only way for this new and life changing healing to come about was to bring up my past traumas once more. He took on His wounds that I may touch, that I may be healed.

When Jesus lifts His upper tunic, revealing the opening in His side, I don't know how to describe it other than it's Heaven and earth at their meeting place. I'm in awe of His torn human flesh, now glorified. *How can something so fatal be so beautiful?*

I encounter Him in His deepest wound as He encounters me in mine and it dazzles me.

Surrounded by the gashes from His scourging, which are now smooth white scars, this Divine Tear in His human side is like a tabernacle waiting to be opened. Pulling back His flesh, Jesus reveals His beating heart to me. He gently moves my trembling hand toward His side, inviting me to place my stained fingers into His very being.

This invitation and His vulnerability are breathtaking.

Sacred Wounds

Pulling my hand back, I still don't feel worthy. "I... I can't. I've doubted all this time, and I still doubt even though I see You." Jesus doesn't look hurt or scandalized by these words, He looks proud of the bravery it took for me to speak them.

"Thomas, thank you for your honesty. I have always loved this about you. Even when others call you a doubter, you do not give in and pretend to believe because of what they say. In your doubt you sincerely wonder, wholeheartedly seek. And you willingly admit that on your own, you cannot believe. I am honored that you have always been honest with Me. All of you is welcome here, especially this part of your heart."

Opening His side, He extends the invitation once more. I reach out my hand, and this time it's not met with emptiness. As I place my palm within Him, I can feel my fingers becoming holy, glorified, anointed. Set apart for some great purpose that doesn't seem so impossible anymore.

Jesus speaks again, "You have always thought your doubting made you weak, but My Father sees it as one of your greatest strengths. You question things, you ponder before you act, you seek to understand the whole picture. It is *because* of these qualities, not in spite of them, that you are an irreplaceable member of My Kingdom, an unrepeatable son of My Father.

"When I look at you, this is who I see. A man seeking faith to move mountains, even when finding that belief seems impossible. Others may call you doubting Thomas, but not Me. I call you faithful Thomas. Patient Thomas. Brave Thomas. It is by these names that I called you forth into being, and by these names that I call you Mine once again. My brother, let your true identity be restored."

As He speaks, I feel as though I'm coming fully alive. Looking at His face, I know these words He breathes over me are true. As my identity sinks in like the deepening roots of a new tree, I know that He'll always be with me, even when I doubt again.

When I've received this stunning gift in its entirety, I slowly draw my hand out, overwhelmed by His goodness. Jesus knows me and loves me so well.

With tenderness in His eyes, Jesus continues to speak. "Thomas, there are many souls who will have a hard time believing in Me, as you did, when they can no longer see Me. But through your budding faith, your magnificent story, your anointed hands, I will work through you to mold their hearts. Because you have touched and you have felt, you can describe My glorious wounds in a way that no other soul can. Because you have personally been set free by My wounds, you can share your testimony and lead others to their own intimate encounter with Me. And it will be to your great joy, My brother!

"Through your unbelief, many will come to believe.

"There will be many more moments when your faith is shaken, but do not be afraid, Thomas. You do not need to have unshakable faith to build My Kingdom, only unrelenting trust. I will be with you, I will work through you. There is so much more glory to come that I cannot wait to show you.

"My brave Thomas, I am so proud of you."

With tears in my eyes I fall to the ground in adoration. Looking into the gaze of Love Himself, I speak the words that I know will forever be on my lips.

"My Lord and my God."

Without a doubt, I know who He is. Without a doubt, I know who I am to Him. And I can't wait to help others come to know Jesus my Brother, too.

Jesus pulls me into a deep embrace. He is my safety. I'm so grateful that He called me all those years ago in the synagogue and I'm so glad I said yes to following Him. All of the sufferings along the way that seemed impossibly cruel were *for me*, a means to deeper intimacy, deeper healing, deeper fulfillment. A means to this very moment of the healing of my identity and being called to an irreplaceable mission.

Jesus puts His arm around my shoulder and together we look out from the balcony at the broad valley. My eyes look from the tree by my childhood home to Calvary hill where His cross once stood. Understanding the bigger picture now, I smile, feeling a lightness in my soul that I haven't felt since before my brother's death.

Yes, these views still remind me of death, but now I know that it doesn't stop here. In Jesus, all death is a means to new life. This is just the beginning.

We hear a sudden burst of celebration from inside the upper room and I can't wait to join in. Without saying a word we walk toward our brothers. Jesus reaches out, opening the unlocked door.

THE BROKEN STAFF

John 18:15-18, 25-27; John 21:7-19; Matthew 14:22-33; Luke 5:1-11

I stare blankly into the pulsing coals. The glowing hues of reds and oranges slow, dwindling. Someone needs to throw another log onto the flame, but I don't move. I no longer feel capable of even such a menial task.

The other disciples are laughing around me, but I hardly hear them. I only hear my own heart pounding in my ears and my blood pulsing through my body. I shiver, though I don't know if it's because I'm afraid or because I'm dripping wet. Maybe both. My body cries for me to draw closer to the warm fire in these early morning hours, closer to Him. But I can't. The small flames remind me too much of the other fire.

I shutter, trying to distract myself from my thoughts. There's more laughter around me and I play along like I heard the joke, like I'm still part of this community. I can't look Jesus in the eyes as a fake smile spreads across my face, so instead I watch His hands. Large and gentle, they prepare the fish He caught for us. As He cleans them, I feel gutted, too.

I haven't spoken to Jesus since His death, since the night in the garden, since the night around the last fire. I don't know why I'd been hoping when I saw Him this morning I'd feel some sort of relief, as if nothing had happened. Because how could He forget such a betrayal? I feel a tangible tension between us, and it's all my fault. I denied Jesus during that pivotal hour and now things can never be the same.

Looking back into the dying coals, I see myself in them. Once filled with blazing passion for the unique mission He called me to, I'm now holding on by a thread. Hardly a spark is left.

My eyes wander to a nearby pile of firewood and suddenly my body freezes. A chill runs down my spine and my breath catches in my throat. Panicking, I see something I hoped never to see again, a reminder of my gravest failure.

My broken staff.

It's scattered among the other pieces of kindling wood, ready to be thrown onto the fire. I recognize the carvings deeply etched in the wood, I'd know them anywhere because I made them with my own two hands. I wince, remembering the sharp snapping sound of the staff as it broke.

Suddenly my mind is slammed with a wave of fearful memories from that night. I have to clear my throat, eyes brimming with tears, as I remember. Judas' betrayal in the garden, the soldiers shouting, Jesus being dragged away in chains. My fear overtaking me, following Jesus at a distance, the uncertainty of what was about to take place. My tightly drawn shawl, the shadows of the fire dancing across my face, the others who would soon recognize me.

What's happening? Where are they taking Him? Should I follow?

I remember the wave of questions had hit me like a tsunami as I clung to my staff, trying to decide, trying to understand. I wanted to defend Him, I told Him I would. But as soon as the soldiers and slaves around the fire started asking me questions, I was overcome with fear.

"Aren't you one of His disciples?" "You were with Jesus the Galilean." "Surely, you know Him!"

Their accusations flew at me like daggers and I chose to protect myself.

"I'd never be one of that Man's disciples!" "How dare you associate me with that Criminal!" "I do not know this Man, Jesus!"

My words still ring in my ears, the shame still echoes in my heart. I'd been such a coward, and I knew it. But it wasn't until the cock crowed three times that I truly recognized the gravity of my failure. In that moment I'd looked over to Jesus and our eyes met just before He was dragged inside. *He heard everything.*

I haven't been able to look Him in the eyes since.

Moments later when His tortuous cries flooded from inside the walls, I started running. Away from the fire, away from my failure, away from myself. I wasn't far when I'd tripped over a rock and hit the hard ground. That's when I heard the snap. The darkness of the night was so thick that I could hardly see what was right in front of me. I frantically groped in the darkness for my staff, and my hands were met by the two pieces of wood.

Shattered. Broken. Severed.

In the pitch blackness I could imagine Jesus standing over me, my broken staff in His hands, denying me in return. *"You'll never live up to the call I have for you, Simon."* His voice felt so real that it still sends a shiver down my spine. I threw the broken pieces of wood into the bushes that night and I'd continued to run. Now, looking at my useless staff on the pile of firewood, probably unknowingly gathered by one of the other disciples, I wonder if Jesus wants to toss me into the fire, too.

I feel like an idiot. For that night, and for this morning, too. What was I thinking, jumping off the boat a couple of minutes ago? Did I really think it could make some sort of a difference? When John yelled out that Jesus was on shore, I dove into the waves without even thinking. I wanted to get to Him, to show Him my devotion once again. But as I paddled against the current I saw a crow fly overhead and up toward the mountain, reminding me of what I'd done. I felt defeated and wished I could sink under the surface and never come back up. The boat beat me to shore, my clothes are dripping wet, and I still can't look at Him.

The fish are ready to be baked in the fire now, and I watch Jesus reach for more kindling wood. As His hand hovers over my broken staff, fear pulses throughout my entire body like a tidal wave and I'm suddenly on my feet, running away from Him once again. *Where am I supposed to go? What am I supposed to do?* I could take a boat, but the others would follow me. And even if I sailed it to the ends of the sea, I still couldn't escape my shame. Looking around frantically, I notice a trail that leads up into the mountain and I begin to sprint.

Tears blur my vision as I go. I run with abandon, chasing a feeling of relief that seems just out of reach. I'm not sure how far I run, but it feels like miles. My sides burn, my feet ache, my heart grieves. When the path below me suddenly changes from dirt into hard rock, I slow. Stepping onto the stone I find myself at a clearing that overlooks the Sea of Galilee.

My feelings are mixed and my gut feels twisted. The waters I know so intimately, the ones I've grown to love, gently dance in the morning

The Broken Staff

sun. I want to remember the warm summers on the sea, catching fish with my dad and brother. But all I can think about is the day Jesus called me – "I will make you a fisher of men" – and how I've let Him down every day since.

I feel ashamed. What must He think of me now? I was supposed to be His rock, His brother, His best friend. But I failed Him when He needed me most. Three years ago when Jesus called me to be a fisher of men, it was as if He called me out to walk upon the waters with Him. But I fell beneath the surface, over and over again. He always came to my aid in the past, but this time the weight of my denials feels like a sinking anchor tied around my shoulders. *This time I've gone too far.* Ever since that Thursday night by the last fire, I feel like I've been treading water and it's only a matter of time until I sink.

Although the morning air is clear and peaceful, the inner turmoil I wrestle with makes me feel like I'm still floating out in the open sea with no vessel in sight and raging storms around me. I'm floundering and I'm afraid. It feels like the waves shove me under the surface, beating me down on all sides. I can't catch my breath.

As panic fills my lungs, I remember how I felt the day Jesus called me. It was an intriguing invitation, an exciting possibility. A great mission, calling me out of the comfort of my fishing boat to stand on the waters with Him. In that moment I wanted nothing else. At first I was comfortable standing out on the open sea with Him. I'd been fishing for as long as I can remember, so I had no fear of the water.

After I gave my "yes" I saw miracles. People healed, lives transformed, even my mother-in-law was restored to health. It all felt so safe and sturdy. I was part of something new. In those beginning days it was as if, standing out on the waters, I could look down and watch my feet press into the blue and green ripples of the sea without being afraid.

Giving my "yes" was like lifting my eyes to Jesus and keeping my gaze on Him as we walked across the waters.

His miracles and teachings were so resounding in that time of our mission that I felt like I could even dance across the sea. I was so focused on Him, my sturdy pillar, a guiding light among the winds, that I could see nothing else. No one else. It was as if the waves beneath me were solid ground.

But then Jesus started to reveal more to us. He spoke with authority, sharing His true identity with us as the Son of God. He spoke about being killed, and how we'd suffer with Him. It was in that moment that my worry started to grow and it soon became my constant companion on the waters. I knew Jesus could calm the storms, I'd seen Him do it with my own eyes. But that was when He was here. *If He has to die, what are we going to do when He's gone? What weight of responsibility will fall on my shoulders?*

The fear began to overwhelm me, and it felt as if I were constantly drowning internally. As my fears of the future grew, my eyes slowly shifted away from Him. Soon my focus was on the storms around me, and the storms that were to come. As my worries weighed me down, my feet began to slip beneath the surface of the sea and before I knew it I was submerged. The more I looked, the more raging storms I saw that I would have to try to handle without Him. I couldn't catch my breath.

I still can't.

And then Jesus died. And my denials of Him that night are the sinking anchor pulling me further below the surface than I've ever

The Broken Staff

been before. I never used to be afraid of the sea, but now it terrifies me. My lungs burn, and I physically feel like they're filling with sea water. I never should've said yes to Jesus' call that day! Because now I can't escape the consequences that come with not being able to live up to it.

I just want air – I just want to be at peace again. I hate that these waters that used to be my joy are now my shackles. The monstrous walls of water crash upon me without mercy. These storms are beyond my power. I'll never overcome them and I can't tread anymore. I'm too tired. I'm about to give in, my chains quickly pulling me below the surface to drown me. Lips barely above water, I use my last breath to pray one simple prayer.

Falling to my knees on the boulder cliff I whisper, "Lord, save me!"

The cry of my heart echoes over the Sea of Galilee.

With my face buried in my hands, knees on the rock, I hear soft footsteps approaching. I turn to see Jesus carrying His own staff in His hands as He walks up the dirt path. I immediately avoid His eyes and my heart begins to pound. I'm terrified that I'll have to explain myself to Him. And I'm even more terrified that I won't get the chance. To say sorry, to admit that I know I was wrong, to acknowledge that I broke His trust. I snapped it in half, just like my staff. But I don't have the words within me, and more than that I lack the courage I need to face Him. So I say the only words that I can muster.

"Depart from me, Lord, for I'm a sinful man." My eyes fall to the ground as I speak and I feel my body droop.

I hear Jesus' footsteps slow as He reaches the end of the dirt path. He removes His sandals before stepping onto the rock with me. He walks over quietly and, sitting next to me, He looks out over the waters, too. When I feel His hand on my shoulder I begin to weep.

In frustration, in hopelessness, in inadequacy, in brokenness.

I move my shoulder away from His hand, feeling unworthy of even His touch. In my failure I've created an unbreachable chasm between us. Truly I didn't set out to build the separation, I didn't intend it. But now I can't take it back. I denied my best Friend on the night He needed me most.

Under the rising morning sun, I tighten my fists, digging my nails into my hands. I'm so angry with myself. I felt the same way a couple of weeks ago when I told Jesus that I couldn't let Him go to Jerusalem to die, that I'd protect Him from any sufferings that would come. But He told me in front of the others that I was thinking as man thinks, not as God does. His undeniable command still echoes in the depths of my heart. *"Get behind Me."* I was so confused when He spoke those words to me. I'd really tried to do what was right, I'd sincerely wanted to protect Him. But I just got in the way, again.

If He told me to get behind Him then, what will He say to me now? No doubt words of condemnation and correction, which I deserve. Over and over again I ponder what He must think of me after that night and I feel like I'm back on the sea being tossed by the waves. My thoughts are in tandem with the chaotic storm. I tumble through the crashing tides of my shame. As they shove me under water and hold me there again, I think of all the times I fell short.

Doubting. Blaspheming. Denying.

I've wanted to be obedient to Jesus from the beginning, to do His will. But I can never seem to get it right. Not in the garden when I drew my sword to protect Him, not on the mountain when I offered

The Broken Staff

tents for the prophets to dwell in, not when He was washing my feet and I called myself unworthy. For three years, I never got it right. I never should've stepped out of my boat in the first place.

He used to tell me He was going to build His Church on me, His rock, that I would play an instrumental and irreplaceable role in His plan. But I guess He didn't realize that rocks sink. I've dragged down His mission and message rather than build it up. Through my actions I've disqualified myself and hurt everyone in my path along the way. I have no doubt He regrets calling *me*. Panicking, I feel like I'm sinking again.

He chose the wrong man.

"Peter."

His voice draws me out of the storms and back to the present. I turn and look Him in the eyes for the first time since the denials. It's as if Jesus' hand breaks through the surface of the water and, grasping my own, pulls me out. His gaze reminds me of the truth that He will never stop saving me. As we stand together on the waters once again, I can finally catch my breath. As the storms continue to rage around us, I speak my heart to Him.

"Jesus, please help me."

He puts His hand on my shoulder again and this time I don't pull away. And yet, so many terrifying thoughts still flood my brain like relentless waves crashing down. *"You denied Him not only once, but three times." "You're such a coward, willing only to defend Him when it makes you feel in control." "Some friend you are, abandoning your Shepherd like that. No wonder your staff was destroyed! You could never be like Him."*

"Peter."

When He speaks my name again, the storms of my heart calm. "My brother, tell Me about your storms." His understanding tone softens my anxiety immediately. There's no condemnation here. I see the desire to restore our friendship in His eyes. Tears warm my vision.

How is it that the One I denied wants to hear about what troubles *my* heart?

Gratitude and relief seep into my body as I begin to share the burdens of my soul. I tell Him of the night in the garden, the courtyard fire, the three denials. He already knows, but He listens intently. I tell of all the times along our three-year journey that I tried to help, but always seemed to mess things up and let Him down. I tell Him about the certainty I felt at our last supper that I wouldn't deny Him no matter what happened, but not three hours later I did. Blatantly. *How can I ever trust that I won't do the same thing again?*

In sincerity I share, "Jesus, I don't know how You could use me after all of this." Without speaking a word, Jesus pulls me into an embrace and He holds me as I weep. "I'm so sorry," I barely get the words out between sobs. "I'm so sorry for what I've done."

Jesus, remaining silent and totally present, holds me deeper. He doesn't speak, He allows me to feel. As I cling to Him and He clings back, my focus begins to shift from the storms back to Him. I'm still in disbelief that, after everything, Jesus still wants to embrace me in grace. Suddenly I notice a new sound among the crashing waves. It's clear and steady. Calming. My being stills completely when I realize what I'm hearing.

His heartbeat.

In the ebb and flow of its beating, my mind pulses with renewed memories that I'd somehow forgotten. The long walks and

The Broken Staff

conversations between Jesus and me. Being part of His intimate community. Fishing together on the sea. The day of my call, the nets overflowing, the boat almost bursting at the seams from so great a catch. I'm reminded of all the good He's done for me and the depth of our friendship, but more than that I'm reminded of my identity in Him.

Peter, beloved brother and friend. As the memories flood my mind, my own heart begins to beat in tandem with His.

Jesus looks at me tenderly and says, "I did not call you that day because I had to, Peter. I called you because I wanted to." My heart flourishes at this truth He speaks over me. He continues, "I desire to reveal more fully to you the great commission I have for your life, which will be your utter joy! And your whole story, including your mistakes, is part of it. I do not only want pieces of you, Peter, I want all of you. I love *all* of you.

"In all that you are, I invite you to lead the others once I am no longer here, to be the firm rock foundation that I have always known you to be. I call you to be the shepherd who leads My people, a staff that they can lean on."

At the sound of His words, a deep joy and enthusiasm well up within me. I feel a great desire to step into this role, the excitement I feel helps me to know that I was created for it. For as long as I can remember I've wanted to be a protector, and others have always told me that I'd make a great leader. It's as if I can see my call clearly for the first time. And yet, I still fear that I'll take the wrong steps yet again, that I'll sink below the waters, dragging everyone with me. Anxiety and hesitation quickly begin to choke my anticipation.

And how am I supposed to be a shepherd if I don't even have a staff?

Looking out over the calm sea as the peaceful day is waking up, I speak my fear aloud to Jesus.

"But what if I fail again when the next storm comes?"

"You will."

His words surprise me. I wait for a moment, expecting Him to laugh. He's joking, right? But when Jesus stands and looks me in the eyes once more, I know He's not.

"The storms will come, Peter. And you will take your eyes off of Me and you will be afraid. You may find yourself beneath the surface again. But Peter, one thing I know about you is that you never give up. You are faithful, even when you do not feel it. Yes, you fell, you denied Me three times, but look where you are. You swam to the shore, you called out to Me. You repented. You always begin again and I love that about you.

"I have always seen the good desire in your heart to honor Me. But I want to free you from the false perception that honoring Me means avoiding failure and always being perfect. I want you to know that no matter how many times you fall, I will always be here to help you up. You will never disappoint Me away from you. My love is not going anywhere. I will never leave you, Peter. When you cry out to Me, I will always be here to lift you out of the waves of the storm.

"I allow these storms for your growth. In your failures, I strengthen you, further preparing you for this mission of joy. Each time you fall, you get up more quickly, even though you cannot perceive it. You see your failures as disqualifying while I see them as a means to draw you closer to My heart. With each fall and each renewal of relationship with Me, our intimacy grows and so does My Kingdom."

The Broken Staff

I feel a deep sense of relief, as if the anchor chains have been broken and I've been relieved of their burden. My deep gratitude and excitement for my call burst forth once more and I feel an undeniable desire to renew my "yes" to Jesus' call over my life. By the deep smile that spreads across Jesus' face, I know my joy is His joy, too. He sees my eagerness to live out this mission, my desire to honor Him has been renewed.

With a smile in His eyes, Jesus speaks again. "There will be many more storms, My brother. You will want to understand them. You will want to control the situations and have power over them. But these are false securities. I call you to something higher." He looks at me with kindness and understanding.

"Peter, do you love Me more than these?"

Three days ago I don't know if I would have said "yes", or even that I could say "yes." But now I see that I can't do this on my own. And so I mean it when I say, "Yes, Lord, You know that I love You. I love You more than the desire to be in control."

He replies, "I will provide the resources and the means for you. Feed My lambs."

I don't fully understand what He means or how He can provide for me when He isn't here any longer, but I trust that He'll strengthen and sustain me.

"Peter," Jesus speaks again. "Do you love Me?"

This time I don't hesitate. "Yes, Lord, You know that I love You."

He replies, "I am inviting you into a role that you have been created for. I know that it will be your great joy to lead others. Just as I have tended to you, tend My sheep."

I can feel the excitement building within me. Such a role of importance to lead His chosen people is an incredible honor. He knows my greatest desires and will fulfill them through this call. Having this commission spoken over me is such a gift. Jesus is so kind to me.

A third time He asks, "Peter, do you love Me?"

With His repeating of this question, my soul becomes grieved. I must be lacking something. Is He asking me again because He didn't believe me the first two times? *Have I failed Him again already?* And then it hits me. He's redeeming my three denials. He's allowing me to speak love and truth into the spaces where I once spoke lies. He asks over and over again not to condemn me, but to set me free.

I respond with certainty, "Lord, You know everything. You know that I love You."

Jesus smiles, deeply moved by my declaration. "I am so proud of you and I cannot wait for you to fully receive this gift. To accompany you, I bestow upon you My Holy Spirit to calm your fears and guide your way. Through your openness and dependence, My Spirit will take care of everything. In My Spirit, feed My sheep."

I watch in awe as Jesus extends His staff toward me, placing it in my hands. "Soon I will leave to be with My Father. Peter, I choose you, I commission you to shepherd My chosen people on My behalf."

The staff feels heavy in my hands. Despite everything He's said, I still don't feel capable.

Turning away, I look out over the Sea of Galilee, the one place that has always been a comfort to me. With my attention on the water, I remember once again His first call over my life, this time with a deeper understanding.

The Broken Staff

I'd been fishing all night, catching nothing. Jesus told me to cast my nets on the other side. The ropes almost broke – the boat almost sank – because there were so many fish. Seeing what He had done for me was the reason I said yes to His first invitation. His words still echo in my heart, *"Come, I will make you into the person I created you to be."*

Through His Power, He provides in abundance. When I obey the authority of the Father, my nets overflow. With a renewed confidence in the provision of Jesus and not my own, I receive the Shepherd's staff.

For the first time since the fire in the courtyard, I feel relief. I can breathe easily once again. This staff, unlike the one made with my own hands, is incapable of breaking because it was crafted by Jesus' divine design. Through these three restorations, these three healings, these three calls to shepherd His sheep, Jesus has reawakened within me the desire to grow His Church and bring others into His beautiful pasture. I will gladly lead.

I stare at the sturdy wood in my hands, in awe of its intricacy. "Peter," Jesus says, "Keep trusting in Me, keep walking in My ways. I will guide you and I will do great things through you. When you begin to doubt, cling to this staff. Lean into it, lean into Me. Remember that you will not be alone, even when the storms rage around you."

I smile back at Him. The staff doesn't feel so heavy anymore.

This calling, it's so grand for a simple fisherman. I feel grateful that I was chosen for such a task as this. "Why did You choose me, Lord? I'm the weakest man of all of us..." I ask in curiosity, now aware that His grace will fill in every space where I lack.

"My friend," He replies, "I chose you because I love you and because you are faithful. In your humility you know your dependency on

Me. The best leader is the one who knows he can do nothing in his own power. It is in the moments when you are incapable that I will step in and do great things through you. But most of all, Peter, I have commissioned *you* so that your joy may be complete."

I watch a smile spread across His face, matching my own. He pulls me into an embrace and I hug my Strength. As I let go of Him, I know He'll never let go of me. Standing upon this mountain of rock with Jesus, I feel restored. With His staff in my right hand, I take a deep breath.

"Shall we join our brothers again?" Jesus asks. I nod, watching as He puts His sandals back on. We walk down the mountain together and I no longer feel afraid.

When we arrive, the fire is still low. I watch as Jesus grabs a handful of wood, including my old broken staff, and places it over the dying flames. He breathes upon it and the fire revives immediately. The flames glow brightly once again, orange and red hues dancing in the air. I watch my old staff fuel the flame. By itself it was useless, it could do nothing. But what God chooses and breathes upon produces abundant life. He can use anyone to draw others closer to Himself, to feed the flames of His Church, and to impact God's chosen people for generations to come. Even a fisherman.

Looking around the circle of men, I wonder if any of the other disciples think Jesus chose the wrong man to lead. But no one seems to question the Shepherd's staff in my hands. Instead, I see eyes filled with joy and anticipation, as if this is what they've expected all along.

Jesus passes around baked fish and we feast and laugh together.

Clinging to my new staff, I'm ready.

THE SHATTERED ALABASTER

Luke 7:36-50; John 10:1-18; John 12:1-8; 2 Samuel 12:3

I freeze mid-step. Heart racing and beads of sweat forming, my gaze rushes to the ground.

I'd hoped to come quickly, quietly. I'd planned to leave my gift at His feet and slip out unnoticed. But there are so many more people here than I expected. And they're all staring at me.

With my right hand I pull my shawl more closely around my dirtied face. In my other palm I feel the smooth alabaster flask, which gives me the courage to keep walking forward. Slowly I raise my eyes, looking for the One who drew me here.

Jesus of Nazareth.

My vision is skewed by my tunic and all I see are the other men. Well-dressed dignitaries, wealthy merchants, holy Pharisees, distinguished politicians. My throat tightens, my breathing shallows. *Many of them have paid for my services.* Shame floods every part of my being. *I shouldn't be here...*

Not only does this place remind me of what I used to do and of what I used to be, but it's also dangerous. I can see raging emotion in the eyes of these men who've known me in the hiddenness. They look afraid, like I might tell the whole room about their adulterous acts.

Angry, like they want to permanently silence the potential threat that I am.

I'm terrified, but I have to offer my gift to Jesus. I have to thank Him for what He's done for me.

Tightening my grip around the clay alabaster, I take a deep breath and keep looking. His commoner's sheep-skin vest stands out among the fine silk tunics donned around Him. I feel a slight smile spread across my face as I think of my father, who used to wear similar coverings when he worked in the fields. Jesus is deep in discussion with those surrounding Him. They must be talking about something important, something far too great for my understanding.

The table is so crowded with people, there couldn't possibly be room for another. I feel so out of place here. No one in this room would want me even at their feet, let alone sitting among them. Least of all, Jesus. I long so badly to be met by His gaze again, but maybe it's better this way. I've already caused enough disturbance.

Shifting my eyes back to the floor I move quickly across the room. Rounding the table where He sits, I can feel the weight of a thousand judgmental stares on me all at once. But it's the whispers that are the heaviest.

"What's that dirty prostitute doing here?" "Who does she think she is coming this close to us?" "How dare she approach our table!"

Warm tears blur my vision as I quicken my pace. *You're almost there. Just place the offering at Jesus' feet and leave.* Nearing His chair, my foot catches on the edge of a rug and I stumble. As if in slow motion, the small, valuable jar slips from my dirty fingers. Grasping a second too slowly at the empty air before me, I watch as the alabaster smashes against the tile ground with a forceful crash.

I feel my heart shatter in tandem with the clay.

Priceless oil spills forth and countless dignitaries instinctively pull their bare feet up onto their chairs. It doesn't matter that this pooling perfume is fit for a king, they don't want to be near it because it's been touched by me. Stained. *I wouldn't want to be near me, either.* A deafening silence fills the room and I know for certain that all eyes are on me. I can feel the exuding emotion, as if there's a thousand palmed stones ready to be thrown.

My vision quickly blurs, my cheeks rush with warmth. Hands shaking, mind racing, I stare at the broken jar before me. It had once been whole, holding something beautiful to offer. And now it's useless, tainted, broken. Just like me. *Why did I have to stain this good thing too?*

Overwhelmed with shame, I want to be anywhere but here. For a moment I even wish I was back where I came from. But only for a moment.

It's been seven years since I first stepped into that life I truly knew nothing about. I hadn't intended to join a brothel, I'd quite literally stumbled upon it. I was on my way to the market to spend my last coin. Orphaned, hungry, and alone. I'd fainted from severe fatigue before I could make it there.

There was a woman at my side when I woke up and she'd seemed so kind. There was something off about her eyes, as if they held a tinge of accusation. But I ignored it and instead chose to feel safe with her immediately. She invited me into her home, offering me a seat at her table. For the first time in so long, I felt like I belonged. Since my father's death I'd been starving for affection even more than for food, so I fell for her kindness.

During our meal she treated me like a beloved member of her family, not the orphaned riff raff that I was. But it was the moment that she complimented my hair that I really trusted her. I shudder now, remembering how I even let her comb through it with her fingers like my father used to in the fields. He always used to tell me how much he loved my free-flowing hair, how much he loved me.

It wasn't long until this woman's true intentions surfaced. When I finished eating and stood to leave, now refreshed and filled, she'd grabbed my wrist harshly. Her gentle voice suddenly turned cold and she demanded I pay for the meal I'd just eaten. Her eyes filled with rage when I showed her that I only had a single coin to my name. Grabbing a fistful of the hair she'd just brushed, she roughly pulled me against her chest, locking me in with her grip.

My scalp screamed and I felt cold, sharp metal against my throat. I wanted to scream in fear. But more than that, I wanted to weep in sorrow. I'd just used this knife to eat a meal that made me feel at home after years of loneliness. Yet it had so quickly been turned against me. *How could I have been so stupid to believe this woman actually cared about me? That anyone would care about me ever again?*

She gave me two options. She would turn me over to the authorities for stealing, or I could work to pay for my meal. With my father dead and no brothers to defend me, I couldn't risk the first. I didn't know what kind of work she had in mind, but it seemed like the better bet. I cry, remembering. Part of me thinks I must've had another choice, I should've done something else to get out of there. But in that moment I felt trapped, so I'd stayed.

And then my new life began, if you can even call it a life.

The Shattered Alabaster

It hadn't been so bad at first. The mistress dressed me in fine clothes and costly jewelry. I even felt beautiful when she painted my face with exotic makeup. But when the first man came, drawn to me for my purity and my long, dark hair, I knew for the first time the look of dripping lust. He left smiling, and I was left violated and disgusted with myself.

That was the day I took on a taintedness I knew I would carry with me for the rest of my life.

It was also the day I learned my true worth.

I'd watched the man as he paid for my company with a pile of stained coins. *Stained, just like me.* My only consolation was that now I could pay for my meal and get out of this awful place. At least that's what I'd thought until the mistress took the majority of the pay for herself, putting my small cut of wages in a purse behind the counter. She didn't leave enough to cover that dreadful meal and I was already famished for another. *How will I ever get out of here?*

As I cried myself to sleep that night, wincing in pain, part of me was glad that papa wasn't alive to see what I'd done. What I'd become. He'd probably be ashamed to call me his daughter, now that I'd tainted his image and the family name. And worse yet, I did it over and over again. Though I was used goods now, men still paid a high price for my company because they were drawn to my long, dark hair. And every night I would weep, knowing that the part of me my father used to delight in was now the delight of more men than I could count.

Then my mistress started sending me the rough drunkards. She told me I deserved them and that I should be grateful to her for keeping me off the streets. She often screamed at me, telling me it was my fault that I'm an orphan and a dirty whore. She told me I could leave at any time, and I believed every word.

This is my fault, I chose this for myself.

I wanted to leave, I really did. But when I sat down, starving, to eat the one meal I was given daily, I always decided to stay one more night. For one more meal at this dreadful table.

Soon the already-bland food started to lose its taste. I was completely alone, trapped in this vicious cycle of use. There was no escape for me. I was eating another tasteless dinner one night, after nearly seven years at the brothel, when a devastating truth caught me off guard, sinking in deeply. Tainted as I was, no man would ever take me as his bride. I would never be truly loved again. It was just me and the abuse of these ruthless men until death do us part.

So I decided to end it. The only way out was to take my life. After my last bite of tasteless food, I took a knife from the kitchen table. Cold metal pressed into my flesh once again as I carried it up the stairs to my room. Overwhelmed with fatigue and weighed down by depression, I hardly even made it there. Stumbling over to my fogged mirror, I looked in it one last time.

I hardly recognized myself. Skin and bone, face smeared with makeup, hair tangled and matted. Dirty and stained, irredeemably so. I felt as though I were wearing a crown of thorns, buried deep into my skull, causing an anguish beyond words. Tears streamed down my face as I took in my reflection.

And for the briefest of beautiful moments, I was suddenly and unexpectedly brought back to the fields with my father.

The Shattered Alabaster

It was so real I could feel the open air on my skin again. A pure little girl, deeply happy. The warm sun kissed my little cheeks as I danced among the sheep. My untamed hair bounced loosely over my shoulders as I ran to my father. Like always, he scooped me up and brought me over to the nearby river. While the sheep drank deeply, my bare feet swayed in the cool trickling stream as my father brushed through my hair with his fingers. As he did, he always sang his favorite Scripture story over me. It was a story about a poor man and a little ewe lamb, his most prized possession. As he sang, I always watched his beaming face reflected in the water as he delighted over me. That particular day he'd made me a beautiful crown of wildflowers, and I felt like royalty before him.

What would papa think of me now?

Blinking drowsily, my awareness was brought back to the foggy mirror that framed my reflection. The view of the prostitute I saw was so far from that of the precious little girl I used to be. I was overwhelmed by a severely deep ache in my heart, realizing that I couldn't remember the words anymore that my father used to sing over me in the fields.

What does it matter now anyway? Every part of me has become irredeemably tainted.

I'd wanted to weep, acknowledging the unutterable pain within me, but I had no more tears to give. So I picked up the knife instead. That's when I felt a still, small voice in the very depth of my being say, *put down the knife and go to the window.* It didn't make sense but I felt drawn to obey.

Moving to the window and pushing it open, I breathed in the fresh air deeply. I couldn't remember the last time I'd been outside. My breath caught in my throat, and for the first time in years I was filled with curiosity as a light melody filled the air. Someone was whistling. Their slow, accompanying footsteps also caught my attention. People usually either rushed past the brothel or into it. But these feet were not in a hurry.

The tune sounded like a bird, chirping and fluttering on a bright spring day. My father used to whistle uniquely to each of his sheep, calling their names. I smiled, remembering how they would leap to him in anticipation and delight. I wished he were still here to call me to himself, too.

I'd leaned farther out the window, hoping to catch a glimpse of this passerby. The Man I saw was strolling leisurely, as if looking for someone. As He walked past my window, He slowed and looked up at me. Our eyes met and He smiled deeply for a long, healing moment. For the first time in years I'd been looked upon with gentleness instead of lust. I never thought I'd be looked upon with love again.

Under His gaze, something awoke within me. As He continued on His way into the night, the small voice pulsed through me once again, accompanied by a surge of courage. *You need to follow this Man.*

I quickly grabbed all of my possessions. I didn't have much to carry, just a ragged tunic and the brush my father had given me. In the bustle, I looked in the mirror one more time. My energy and resolve were instantly drained.

All I could focus on was my dirty, tangled hair.

I considered taking the knife and cutting off the one tainted part of me that I could remove. I would've, but there was no time. I had to leave before the whistling Man got too far away. The best I could do was pull my shabby tunic over my head, hiding my hair until I had another chance. Leaving the knife behind, I ran down the stairs, grabbed my purse of earnings from behind the counter and rushed into the frigid night air, closing the door behind me.

By the time I got outside the Man was gone. I spent the night searching the mostly empty streets for Him. It wasn't until dawn was breaking that I saw people running, breathlessly talking about a Man of kindness named Jesus. I knew it must be Him, so I started to run, too. By the time we made it to the courtyard of a wealthy Pharisee, the sun was high in the sky. I was hungry, tired, and thirsting for more than I knew. But when I saw the whistling Man across the crowds, I forgot all of my fatigue.

As hundreds of people pressed upon this Man named Jesus, I took in the scene before me. I saw every kind of illness and disability, every kind of physical embodiment of pain. I'd never seen so many suffering souls at once before, and yet I somehow saw myself in each one of them. But I felt a tinge of jealousy, too. At least these people knew what their ailments were.

My wounds weren't the kind that could be seen. My hurts took residence in the very depths of my scourged heart. Deeply rooted, veiled by shame. My sufferings had been part of my daily life, building year after year, man after man, yet I still didn't know how to put them into words. I didn't know where to begin.

How can Jesus heal me of something I don't even know how to ask Him for?

I began to panic, feeling like I was back at the brothel. Trapped in an endless cycle that I was somehow responsible to get out of, but I had no understanding of where to begin. The more I looked at the crowds, the more I realized I could never be healed and the more I wanted to get away. I don't belong here, either.

I turned to leave, when the still, small voice returned. *Stay. Listen. Receive.*

The crowds grew silent, and one voice rose above the rest. I'll never forget the words Jesus spoke, and how it felt like He was speaking directly to *me*.

"I am the Good Shepherd."

When I heard His words it was as if I was in the field with my papa again. Watching him delight over his sheep, watching him delight over me. The small voice spoke in my heart, *The Father delights over you, too.*

Jesus went on, "A hired man, who is not a shepherd and whose sheep are not his own, sees a wolf coming and leaves the sheep and runs away. This is because he works for pay and has no concern for the sheep."

Your mistress had no true concern for you, beloved one. She used you. But you are worthy of Love, you are worthy of belonging. Your Father loves and cares for you.

"A thief comes only to steal and slaughter and destroy."

The men your mistress forced upon you were thieves. They stole from you and left you feeling stained. Your Father seeks to restore you, He sees your magnificence and He honors you.

"When a sheep gets caught in the thicket, I leave the ninety-nine behind to set the one free."

You were a young sheep caught in the thicket without a trustworthy shepherd. When you cried out, seeking help, you were met with deceit and abuse. But your Father seeks you out because He deeply cares for you. He comes to set you free.

"I am the Good Shepherd, and I know My sheep and Mine know Me."

Your Father knows you. He knows all of your story, and He delights over you.

"My sheep hear My voice. When I call My sheep by name, I lead them out and I walk before them."

Your Father knows you by name. He is doing something new within you. He will lead you. He is with you, always going before you.

"I am the Good Shepherd. A good shepherd lays down His life for His sheep." Jesus' eyes had scanned the crowd before landing on me as He spoke the final words of this deep healing.

"And you are worthy of this extravagant Love. *You are Mine.*"

Even though I had tears in my eyes, I could still see Jesus smiling at me from across the expanse of suffering. For the first time in years, my soul and body were quieted, and I smiled back. Part of me was deeply saddened, knowing that whatever new thing He was doing in my life couldn't involve belonging to His community. There'd be no place for me, no role for a prostitute serving a pure Man like Jesus. I was ritually unclean and I always would be.

But, despite my reality, I had sincere hope that Jesus could still somehow guide my life for good. And my deep gratitude for this truth felt like a bubbling fountain, bursting forth within me. In that moment I decided I would leave town and start anew. But before I did, I wanted to show Jesus gratitude for what He'd done for me. How could I not?

Then I remembered the purse holding my earnings. Coins I could use to buy something!

Without another thought, I bolted from the courtyard and was soon in the nearby market. Having left in such a hurry the night before, I hadn't had a chance to count my earnings. Pulling apart the folds of fabric, I was shocked by the large pile of coins. Swallowing deeply, I finally realized just how long I'd been caught in the thistles of the brothel. With each piece counted, a feeling of shame returned, until it was wrapped tightly around me like the shawl on my head.

That's a lot of coins, a lot of men, a lot of filth...

But I'd just been taught that the Good Shepherd comes among tainted things, and I decided to believe Jesus' words. So I kept walking. The merchant of the most expensive shop in the market almost didn't let me in when he recognized me, not until he saw my spilling pile of coins. When I asked him for the most extraordinary item he had, I was handed the small, sealed flask. This precious and rare oil had been aging for over seventy-seven years. Made of pressed wildflowers, it had been used by people of royal descent. I knew it was the perfect gift to honor Jesus.

Staring at the small, yet extravagant gift in my makeup stained hands, I wished so badly to be like this little alabaster offering. Whole, priceless, and filled to the brim with something good to give. Holding it in my hand, I'd returned to the courtyard of the Pharisee's house and seeing lights on inside, I'd wandered in.

That's when I stumbled into this room of judgment, dropping the one pure thing I had to my name, destroying the only thing I had left to give.

As the stark silence of the room reverberates in my body, I know that I never should've come here. But the mess of fine oil has been made on the floor and I need to clean it up. Kneeling before Jesus, I notice that the rich, spiced smell of revered ointment fills the air. An inescapable reminder of my failure. *So much for royalty...*

My heart wrenches as I think of this ruined gift that I so badly wanted to give and I begin to weep. My makeup stained tears fall onto Jesus' bare feet, the only pair remaining on the ground. I frantically look around the floor, trying to find something to wipe them clean with. But there's nothing, I have nothing.

I hear the still, small voice once again. *Your hair.*

But I can't. My disgusting, mangled, unholy hair is the dirtiest thing about me. Uncovered before so many men, how could it do anything but repulse Jesus?

You are safe to be seen in your fullness by Him.

I've come to trust this voice, so I reach for my shawl, removing it slowly, unveiling my hair like a bride before her groom on their wedding night. The whispers around the table grow louder, but with my decision made, I hardly hear them.

Give your gift of thanksgiving to Him.

Shaking, I take my hair and begin to soak it in the puddle of spilled perfume. The smell overwhelms me, like a fresh field in springtime. I place my dripping hair upon His feet. Jesus doesn't draw away from me, He allows this moment of intimacy to take place. As I continue to weep, my tears mingle with the oil, anointing His feet. These are tears of mourning for what I've been through, tears of gratitude for the healing He's already given, and tears of hope for the healing to come. I savor this moment of closeness with Him.

When I'm finished, I kiss both of Jesus' feet and wrap my hair once again in my dirty tunic.

The whispers around the room escalate to shouts, and the Pharisee whose home we're in speaks on behalf of the others. "Rabbi, if You truly are the Messiah, You'd know what sort of woman is touching You. Don't You know who she is? Don't You know what she's done?"

They can't believe I touched Him. I can't believe it either. Have I made a grave mistake?

I look down at the ground as Jesus speaks. "I know exactly who she is." Is that a smile I hear in His voice? "She is My daughter. She is Mine."

I feel His hand on my chin, gently lifting my face to look at His. I see the same Man I saw from my window and the same Man who healed me from across the crowd. My Shepherd. His eyes are soft, filled with a deep kindness. I instantly feel a peace I've never known before. He holds my hand as He continues speaking to the host.

"I came into your home, and I am grateful to be here. But you did not give Me water to wash My feet. You did not give Me oil to anoint My head. And here is My daughter, My bride, My beautiful guest, who has washed My feet with her tears, dried them with her hair, and anointed them with this costly perfume.

"Her extravagant love has captivated My heart and it will be spoken about for generations."

It's been so long since I was defended, protected. I no longer feel like a sheep without a shepherd. Set free from the thistles, He carries me on His shoulders and calls His neighbors together to celebrate the finding of His lost sheep.

The host looks down, realizing his error. Many of the other men scoff, putting their shoes back on and pushing away from the tables loudly. They leave, not wanting any part in this scandal of love. Once they're gone, only a small group of men and women remain. I take a moment to look from one face to the next, and I'm met with friendliness. The eyes I see are filled with sincere kindness. There is no accusation here. It's obvious that they're glad I'm here, and I smile deeply.

Jesus turns and says tenderly, "Mother." A woman stands from one of the tables. As she makes her way toward me, carrying a basin of water and a clean towel, she hands them to Jesus and they both lead me a little way away from the table. Then the woman removes the blue veil from her own head and wraps it around me, covering my dirty clothes. Before leaving, she looks into my eyes and smiles deeply. Through her gaze, I feel as though I'm being embraced. She squeezes my hand and kisses the top of my head, as if she were my mother, too. I know I'm welcome here.

As I watch what Jesus does next, I forget about everyone else in the room. He dips the clean towel into the water and gently washes the make-up stains off of my face and hands. I'm shocked by how stark the black makeup looks on the white towel. *Did I just stain another good thing?* But as soon as He places the towel back into the water, the black marks dissipate, slowly disappearing from the towel all together.

When all of my makeup has been wiped clean, He asks me a stunningly intimate question.

"May I remove your veil, beloved?"

I hesitate. Though I'm physically clean, I still know I'm stained.

"I don't feel worthy. I stumbled upon my circumstances, but I can't deny the choices I made within them. I never can be fully clean because I chose to stay."

"And I choose you."

In awe, I nod my head, giving Him permission. Jesus slowly places His hands on the stained tunic covering my hair and removes it gently. Just yesterday, before almost taking my life, I felt like I was bearing a crown of thorns, a torture device that was forever a part of me. In this moment I feel as though He's removing it. My mangled hair falls across my shoulders and I look down in shame. But Jesus doesn't hesitate. He reaches for my hair and begins to wash it. As He pours clean water over the years of filth, He brushes His fingers through my hair and He begins to speak over me.

"I know you resonate with the alabaster jar, shattered and seemingly incapable of restoration. But through its brokenness it has become an offering as the gift it was intended to be. A beautiful fragrance now flows freely, filling the whole house with its royal scent. It is not wasted, My daughter – your brokenness is not wasted. It is My honor to hold every piece of your story in My hands and bring restoration."

I weep in pure gratitude. As Jesus prepares my hair for the feast, I can see His reflection in the water basin. He's delighting over me.

When my hair is tangle-free for the first time in years, Jesus cups my face in His gentle hands. With tears in His eyes, He gives His own gift to me. He goes back to where the alabaster was shattered and dips His thumb into some of the remaining ointment on the floor. He walks back to me and crosses me on the forehead. With this holy oil made of pressed wildflowers, it's like He's placing a new kind of crown on my head. I know my royalty before Him.

Jesus speaks again, "You belong here, My love. It is a gift to have you at My table. Be made whole."

Suddenly the Scripture papa used to sing over me in the fields comes rushing back to me in full:

"But the poor man had nothing at all except one little ewe lamb that he had bought. He nourished her, and she grew up with him and his children. Of what little he had she ate; from his own cup she drank; in his bosom she slept; she was like a daughter to him, she was like a daughter to him..."

With a bursting heart I jump into Jesus' arms and embrace Him deeply. I don't know whose smile is bigger, mine or His! I'd been wrong this morning among the ailing crowds, thinking Jesus couldn't heal me. Thinking that I had to be able to put my wounds into words in order to be set free...

Jesus comes among the brokenness, He understands, and He heals profoundly.

Pulling out a chair for me beside His own, Jesus invites me to the table. He introduces me to His community and I'm warmly welcomed in. I'm finally home. Looking around, I can't believe this is only the first of many meals we'll get to share together. And better yet, there's plenty of room at the table for others to join.

As the sweet smell of ointment continues to spread, filling the whole house, we feast and laugh together.

THE UNBEARABLE CROSS

Luke 23:26-46; all Gospel accounts of the Passion

I close my eyes to darkness and open them to chaos.

The storm clouds brew above. Centurions are shouting, their whips are snapping, my body is trembling.

One soldier holds my shaking hands while another roughly cuts through the thick rope that sticks to my raw wrists. For several days I've been twisting, gnawing, trying to fight my way through these fibers to no avail. My efforts hadn't loosened the constraints at all, they'd only further torn open my skin. The once-tan rope is now saturated deep red, dripping with blood. I wince with each cut and pull of the blade.

The moment the knife breaks through, freeing my wrists, I run. But after two steps I stumble to the ground, dizzy from my loss of blood, famished from not eating in days. The soldiers are upon me in seconds, mercilessly kicking my abdomen. I hear one of my ribs snap. Laughing and jeering, the guards don't stop until they're short of breath and wiping sweat from their brows.

Curled up in a ball, vision going dark, I'm too exhausted to resist them in any way. I'm about to give into the relief of blackness when I hear something that feels like another punch in the gut. My brother, face down in the mud next to me, joins them in their laughter. Even through my blurred vision I can see the disgust and taunting in his eyes.

"Good try, little brother. You *almost* got away this time," he sneers.

Though we'd been starved in the same cell for three days, this is the first acknowledgement my brother's given me since our imprisonment. His voice drips with sarcasm, his words sting.

I feel a deeply rooted anger stirring in my heart. I wish I had the courage to turn and spit in his cold, arrogant face. I want to yell, *This is all your fault! You don't care that you're about to walk to your execution, and you don't care that you're taking me with you!* I'm caught off guard by the sudden ache I feel at the core of my being, an inconsolable sadness that goes even deeper than the rage. *You're my big brother. You were supposed to protect me...* I feel my eyes warm with tears. I turn away to avoid further mockery.

Though I'm hurt and angry, I'm not surprised that my brother embraces death with a cold, lifeless laugh. Ever since our mother's death, he's been recklessly seeking out danger rather than avoiding it. Fighting the roughest men, stealing from the richest. Some part of his distorted soul is fed anytime he's mere inches away from a brutal beating. He seems to thrive when he's dancing on cliff's edge, the same place I'm most terrified to be. He constantly seeks out danger, no matter the consequences it has for us. And he always gets caught, leaving us more bloodied and beaten than the last time. Today is no exception.

The throbbing in my wrists pulls me from my thoughts. Warm blood spills forth from the raw flesh and when I see some rope fibers still clinging to my puss-engorged skin, I heave. If I'd eaten breakfast this

The Unbearable Cross

morning it would be all over me. I close my eyes tightly, hoping the urge to faint will return.

The nothingness of death will be an immense relief.

I black out momentarily from a sudden, rough jerking movement. Vision blurry, ears ringing, I realize the soldiers have yanked us from the ground and pulled us to our feet. Hardly conscious, I hear what sounds like cloth being torn. The sudden whip of biting wind against my bare thighs pulls me back to awareness. They've ripped off our tunics, the ones our mother gave us, leaving us in nothing but thin loin cloths.

There's an uproar of laughter from the gathering crowd. My brother, undaunted by their jeers, laughs back with an unwavering hardness in his eyes. I lower my gaze to the ground, overcome with shame. The freezing air numbs my naked skin. I don't know if I'm shivering from the cold or from embarrassment.

My stomach groans as my hands shake violently from the pain. My brother laughs again.

How long will this public humiliation last?

I hear a deep rumbling overhead as a wall of eerie black clouds billow in the darkening sky. A similar feeling fills my chest as I take in the overwhelming sight before me. Three soldiers walk toward me carrying a massive wooden beam. Centurions are known for their physical strength, but even they struggle under its weight. I can see the sweat on their brows.

When they throw it across my shoulders, the crushing weight punches the air out of my lungs. The rough texture pounds against my neck and back mercilessly I almost don't feel anything for a moment and then, torture. My entire body pulses, my skin screams as if I'd just gotten ten thousand splinters at once. I gasp for air as I watch the soldiers throw my brother's wooden beam upon his back.

We haven't even begun and I'm already crushed by the weight of my cross.

I cry out in pain as they bind my exposed wrists to the splintering wood with a new thick rope. *You don't need to do that,* I want to yell, *my oozing skin sticks to the beam on its own!* They pull so tightly that the fibers start to fray. I writhe in pain.

When the soldiers step back, letting the full weight of the wood rest on my shoulders, the sheer heaviness is overwhelming. My upper body slowly collapses, pushing deeply into my hips. My lungs fold, my breathing shallows fiercely. I feel like I'm being buried alive.

Am I just imagining it, or is the heavy beam screaming at me as it pushes my feet into the ground? Or is that my brother's voice?

"Without help, you'll never be able to carry the unbearable weight of your cross!"

Whoever it is, I know they're right. If three strong guards struggled to lift it, how can I – beaten and starved – possibly muster the strength? My whole body convulses, my entire being screams at my devastating reality. I'm supposed to carry my cross all the way to the hill. I'll never make it.

I would give anything to be anywhere other than this way of the cross.

Tears of terror and resignation roll down my face, mingling with my blood and the cold rain that now falls. I feel so utterly alone. Even though I know she can't hear me, I yell out to the only person who would care about my immense suffering.

"Mama, please hold me!"

The crowds erupt in laughter again, but this time my brother doesn't join in. Our eyes lock. Is that sadness that tinges the hardness of his eyes? As our legs violently tremble in tandem, I hope he can read the begging questions my own eyes carry.

What happened to us, brother? How did we get here?

I can still taste the dust, mingled with the scent of fresh bread. It hung in the air on that thick summer day. The first time we stole. The market bustled loudly, warm sweat dripped down my lower back, and I'd cleverly distracted the baker while my brother snuck two fresh loaves into his satchel. The bread had been steaming and I'd been afraid someone would see the heat escaping from his bag and catch us.

We almost got away with it, but then we passed the cart of fine jewelry.

Sheer terror ran down my spine as I watched my brother. He subtly guided a large red ruby from the jeweler's stand into his bag without missing a step. *What was he doing? We hadn't planned this. Getting caught for stealing bread would get us a stern lecture, but this was different. This was dangerous.* As the jewel slid into his bag beside the bread, it caught the sun, glimmering scarlet. My entire body had tingled, the hair on my neck stood at full attention as the truth sunk in.

We'd just become robbers.

That was the first time I'd asked myself the same question I'm still wondering today. *We were just hungry kids in need of food. We didn't want to be thieves, right, big brother?*

I'd trusted my brother on that warm, sticky day. So when he kept walking, fresh bread and blood-red ruby hidden at his side, I kept walking too. It didn't take long for the stand-owner to realize his most prized possession was missing, to gather a motley crew of merchants, and to track us down. It didn't matter that we were just kids. They took us outside of town and beat us until we were dripping ruby red. The jeweler's terrifying voice still haunts me. "That'll teach you never to steal again!" I'd learned my lesson that day. I just wish my brother had, too.

Such a young boy, I was left traumatized and shaking. My only solace in that moment was knowing my big brother was there to protect me, to pick me up and carry me to safety.

But he didn't.

Instead, he got in my face and screamed, *"Oh boo hoo, stop crying for Mom. She's dead!"* That was the moment I watched his once gentle and playful eyes turn hard. I haven't seen them since. He'd kicked dust in my bruised and bleeding face before walking back to town without me. It was as if he'd shoved a knife right into my already aching heart, twisting it harshly.

That was the only time I ever considered leaving him. But the last words my mother spoke haunted me. *"No matter what happens, stay together. Take care of each other, all the way to the end."* I couldn't deny my mother her dying wish, so that day I decided to stay with him no matter what might come. That was the moment I grew up, and in that instant my carefree childhood was stripped away from me.

Every time my brother stole after that – each week something more exquisite, earning a graver beating – he twisted the knife in my heart ever-deeper. Having no choice but to bear the beatings with him, I constantly wished we'd get arrested. Prison felt safer than being in my brother's care. My wish came true three days ago when the Roman officials finally imprisoned us. Now, I can't tell which reality is worse...

Sheer pain pulls me back to the present moment.

Feeling something warm spilling across my bare chest, I turn my head to see more blood. The movement sends a searing pain from my neck to my fingertips and I cry out. I see something silver, gleaming. When I realize it's a thick, dull nail sticking out of the wood and digging into my shoulder, my vision begins to darken and I feel my body sway. I close my eyes tightly, wishing it all away. I begin the way to my crucifixion and the nail sinks deeper with each step, in seconds it's rubbing against my bone.

I try to catch my brother's gaze again, hoping to find some emotion there. But he won't look at me. He curses and spits at a soldier before taking his first steps toward Calvary. My whole being shakes. My shoulders throb. Course splinters scuff my chafed skin. My soul groans, I'm ready to give up and we've only just begun. Even though my brother walks next to me, I feel completely alone.

It's early afternoon, but the sky has grown dark, bringing an unshakable chill with it. My teeth chatter in tandem with the falling rain and my loincloth whips against my numb flesh. Exhausted, I look down the long road ahead of us, all the way to the hill. It's nothing but endless cobblestone for miles. Through the thick sheets of rain, I almost don't notice the Figure a long way ahead of us. He's also carrying a cross, but His is made of two beams instead of one. He's moving slowly, as if His feet are weighted stones dragging Him down.

I don't understand the meaning, but I hear the crowds in the distance yelling, "King of the Jews." For a moment I pity the Criminal. *I can't* fathom carrying twice the amount of weight, experiencing twice the amount of excruciating pain. But when He slips and falls, I feel a chuckle leave my chest. *Or maybe He's like my brother and He deserves everything He's getting.* Even from a distance, His body hitting the hard stones with no resistance sounds like another clap of thunder.

When my brother hears me laugh, he smiles and laughs too. It's the first time he's ever followed me in anything and I feel dirty. I wish I could take it back. I don't want to be like him in any way. *But what does it matter now? We're walking to our deaths. Condemned, publicly humiliated, forever damned. It's too late to be anything else and it's all his fault.* My anger stirs like the rumbling clouds above us, ready to spill over.

We stagger on for what seems like hours in the cold, pounding, relentless rain. The pain is unbearable. The only reason I keep going is because I know it'll be worse if I stop. The guards won't give me the respect of killing me on the spot. They'll only scourge me with their glass-strewn whips before forcing me back to my feet. Knowing this, I still consider stopping, lying down, and taking an extra beating anyway. *Maybe I'll get lucky and they'll accidently kill me with a brutal blow.*

But then I imagine my mother being here, watching the torture that would occur. What they'd do to me would kill her if she weren't already dead. For the first time in my life, I'm glad she's gone so she doesn't have to see me like this, *to see what I've become.* A tear slides down my face as we slowly continue forward. The only solace is the eternal darkness of death waiting for me on the hill.

I don't know how long it's been when we approach a group of soldiers huddled around a body laying in the middle of the road. I hear the phrase "King of the Jews" again. It must be the Criminal carrying two beams who seemed miles ahead of us hours ago. He must've fallen again. The guards are yelling back and forth to one another. I can hardly hear them through the pouring rain, but I hear enough. They aren't going to let us pass this Man, they're going to make us wait for Him.

I almost collapse at the idea. My body is caked in blood, skin chafed and raw from the cold. The nail in my flesh pushes deeply into bone, the weight of the wood on my shoulders is suffocating. I can't stop for Him! I grow enraged at this Criminal on the ground. *Why should I suffer because You're too weak to keep going? It's clear from Your cruciform beams that You've done something much worse than us. I'm sickened to even be associated with You, You maggot!* I wish I had the breath to say it aloud.

When my brother realizes what's happening, I hear him curse the Man under his breath. I open my mouth to join him and the crowds and I yell as loudly as my decaying body can muster, "All hail, the King of the—"

But I can't finish my sentence.

The soldiers move away from the Man on the ground. *Can He even be called a Man anymore?* I'm horrified by the picture I see. The Man's entire back is open flesh, shredded skin. I can see it pulsing and I almost scream. The white of His spine is stark in the sea of red. It's surrounded by torn ligaments, blood, and nothing else. Deep, thick fluid seeps from every crevice of His being. I didn't even know the human body contained so much blood.

The Criminal turns His face toward us and I almost faint. The only features I can make out are His yellowed eyes and open mouth, labored breathing on His lips. A single tear rolls down where His cheek should be. He reeks of sweat and waste and blood and torn human flesh. The rough wood of His cross meshes with the purple bruises and ivory bones that compose His body. It's as if His skin and the cross have become one flesh. This Man's sufferings are unimaginable, inexpressible. It's as if He bears the sins of a thousand thieves. Though He looks more like a worm than a Man, there's something familiar about Him.

I'm in shock. I want to look away, I want to run.

And then He looks right at me.

I stare at Him and I begin to weep as it sinks in. *He looks so familiar because, looking at Him, I see the embodiment of exactly how I feel.* It's like I'm looking in a mirror. Abandoned, exposed, beaten, torn. A brother, with no one to save him. A son afflicted before his mother. A sheep led to the slaughter. *His entire identity has been stripped away, leaving behind a bloodied, desperate, hurting orphan.*

I wince in pain, noticing the torture device wrapped around His head. A crown of some sort. *Are those thorns?* It's shoved deeply into His skull and my own head throbs at the sight. It must be a symbol of mockery, maybe something to do with why everyone keeps calling Him "King." *What could this Man possibly have done?*

Staring into His eyes, I wonder if He's a robber who isn't responsible for the cross He carries, either.

Without even knowing why, I take a step toward Him. He has tears in His eyes, too. Somehow I know that in the midst of His unutterable suffering He's not crying for Himself. No, He's crying for me in my own suffering. And for the first time since my mother's death, I don't feel alone. I don't know who this Man is, but there's something different about Him.

He doesn't look away and neither do I.

And I continue to weep. For myself, for the little boy who's lost so much in his lifetime, who was just trying his best. I grieve the early loss of my childhood, my innocence. I mourn the recent years, full of fear and thievery, spent trying to keep my word.

"Don't worry, Mama, I'll never leave him. He's my brother."

I hadn't realized until this moment just how broken my story has left me. For so many years I've just been trying to survive. But finally I see my shattered, broken self reflected in the face of this Man. And it means everything to me. There's something about this Criminal that draws me to Himself. I speak to Him through my broken breaths, caused by the weight of my cross. "I don't know... if You deserve this torture... but I'm... sorry You're suffering... You're not alone..." For a brief moment, He looks consoled.

I feel consoled, too. I feel known. I feel like I have a Brother again.

I open my mouth to say more, but I'm nearly knocked off my feet by a centurion. He shoves by carrying a thick branch in his hands. He gets in the Criminal's face and taunts Him before using the stick to shove the crown of thorns even more deeply into His flesh. As if I feel the pain myself, I yell out. My cry echoes that of the Man in agony. The soldier laughs bitterly as fresh blood pours forth. He roughly grabs the Man's arm, fingers sinking into open wounds, and pulls Him to His feet.

I hear a woman cry out. Looking to the crowds, I see her shoving her way toward us. The soldiers are trying to keep her at bay, but when the Man beside me falls again, nothing can stop her. Like a protective mother bear, she fiercely runs to her threatened cub. Sobbing, she cradles His face in her hands. I have no idea who she is, but it's clear that her heart is breaking in tandem with His. Their eyes lock as she holds His bloodied face in her hands, wiping His tears with her fingers. As she clings to Him, my vision blurs again. I wish my mama was here to hold me...

I'll never forget the last time I was in her arms, she was kissing my newly bruised knee. Her cries of fear filled the open air when I fell from the tree. I can still see her look of tender love and overwhelming concern as she ran toward me. It didn't matter that she'd told me not to climb that tree a thousand times, she was just glad I was okay. That's my last memory of my mother, and being in her arms was the safest I ever felt.

Part of me feels jealous to see this tortured Man, held. I almost look away. But I'm drawn into this intimacy that I so deeply desire for myself. For the briefest moment, the woman turns her gaze and looks right at me. Her eyes are kind, loving, empathetic. In the midst of the chaos, I somehow feel peace. Despite the distance between us, I feel like she's embracing me, too.

Just as quickly as this peaceful moment came, it's gone. The woman's weeping fills the air again as the soldiers yank at her tunic, trying to pull her away. She pushes their arms away one last time and kisses the Man's face over and over again until she can't resist the guards any longer. When they pull her away her hands and face are stained red.

"My Son!" she sobs. "My little boy, Jesus, keep doing whatever Your Father tells You. I love You!"

As if her words pierce the sky as deeply as they pierce my own heart, there's a terrifying crash of lightning and the wild rains begin to pour again. Another woman in the crowd pulls this beloved mother into an embrace and their cries fill the air.

I look back to this Man called Jesus. With His gaze on His mother, He does everything in His power to simply stay on His feet. Swaying with the wind, His body shakes violently. His eyes begin to roll back and I'm afraid He'll fall again.

I feel my brother hiss in my ear, "Push... Him... over!"

His breathing is so shallow he can hardly get out more than one word at a time. I stare at him, disgusted. Has his heart really become so hard that he prefers cursing others to saving his last breaths? My brother's eyes are still hard, and a dark smile spreads across his face as he waits for my response. I know he's expecting me to do whatever he tells me, like I've done since the day he stole that ruby. But look where that's gotten us.

"No!"

My brother stares at me, shocked. I've never yelled at him before. But now that I've started, I won't stop.

"This Man hasn't... done anything to... hurt me... I should be... pushing *you* over... you're the one... who brought us here... *brother*." I say the last word harshly, a slap in the face that I hope stings. Now I begin to understand why he wanted to use his lingering breaths to curse. I continue, "This is all... your fault... I'm glad Mama's dead... so she doesn't have to see... what you've become!"

As soon as the last words leave my mouth I know they were too far. For a split second I see hurt in my brother's eyes, but it quickly turns to rage. He charges at me with the full weight of his cross. I lose my balance when he hits me, but I stay on my feet. A clap of thunder slams overhead and it's as if it stokes ablaze the rage in my heart. Emotion rips through my being like the pain that envelops it.

I'm so angry!

Angry at my mother for dying, for making me promise to stay with my brother, for trusting him to take care of me!

Angry at my brother for chasing after riches instead of my safety, for turning from my best friend into my gravest threat, for leading us to this unbearable suffering!

Angry at God, if He even exists, for giving us only two options that day – thievery or starvation, for abandoning us, for turning us into robbers that our mother would be ashamed of!

But mostly I'm angry at myself, for being stupid enough to follow along. I should've left my brother the day he stole the ruby!

I look at my brother and yell with every fiber of my being as I charge at him. Pain rips through my body on impact but I don't care. I slam his sternum with my cross as hard as I can. He trips and falls face down onto the hard cobblestone. He stays on the ground for a long time. I scoff. *Maybe he's dead, I hope he is.*

I look over to Jesus to see if He's laughing too, but His eyes are filled with pain. It's as though I'd just done to Him what I'd done to my brother. My heart sinks. I see myself reflected in this tortured Man, Jesus, but it isn't until this moment that I see my brother reflected in Him, too. Though my emotions of hurt and anger are valid, I realize I've never tried to understand my brother's actions, his hurt. *He lost our mama, too...* I suddenly hope I have the chance to ask him before we die.

Two soldiers pull my brother to his feet. There's a large, fresh gash across his forehead. I see something else, too. Embarrassment, shame, belittlement. He looks like the little boy he really is, being crushed by the weight of the world on his shoulders. Hardly able to breathe, I limp over to my brother. I place the wood of my own cross under his and I push upward with all of my strength, hoping to give him some relief. I almost blackout from the new rush of pain, but I stay by him until he catches his breath. Blood from his cross drips onto mine.

Catching his slightly softened eyes I don't have the breath to say I'm sorry, but I think he sees it in my gaze. I hope he does.

I look to Jesus and I watch as He embraces His cross with His shaking body. I do the same and we all continue on. The rain pounds, my body screams. The pain is so excruciating that the series of events that happens next may have taken mere moments, but it feels like hours. A man being pulled from the crowd to help Jesus carry His cross. How quickly he became stained red, too. The group of women mourning for Jesus as we passed them. His mother close by, weeping silently.

Blood. Flesh. Sin. Death.

It's overwhelming.

I have no idea how we made it here, but we've completed our final, excruciating ascent up the hill. Now we're on Calvary and the freezing rain pounds against our naked, bleeding beings. When the man who was helping Him gets pulled back into the crowds, I watch Jesus shake violently under His cross. His dying body falls for the last time into a pool of His own blood. He's crushed under the weight of the wood. A group of soldiers surround Jesus, kicking Him relentlessly, mocking Him mercilessly.

"Some king, huh?" I hear one yell, causing an uproar of laughter. "Bow down, everyone, to the Messiah!"

Messiah?

My mind floods with the scripture stories our mother used to read to us. *"There will be a Messiah! He'll save us and take us to His Kingdom!"* Could this really be the One we've been waiting for?

A startling flash of lightning strikes and the light catches on a piece of metal sticking out of Jesus' cross. *What is that?* I squint my eyes, trying to focus my ever-blurring vision on the little piece of silver. It's a long, dull nail. I look to Jesus' shoulder and see a severe puncture, deep enough to hit bone. The nail must've been digging into his shoulder this whole time, like the nail on my own cross was digging into mine.

He is carrying my cross, my sufferings on His shoulders.

In that moment I recognize my Messiah hidden behind the veil of torn flesh. I know without a doubt that He is Love. He's not just another thief, but the Thief of Death. Our Savior, the One we've been waiting for. They've been calling Him "King of the Jews" but He really is the King of kings.

I immediately fall to my knees in reverence. As the soldiers and bystanders around me get on their knees and pay Him mocking homage, I bow my head in respect. *Who am I to be on the same way of the cross as our Savior, to have my blood intermingle with His?*

Our eyes lock and I accompany Jesus in the only way I can – I don't look away from the holy ground of His suffering or of mine. I recognize His sacredness and I honor Him. As I look into the face of Love Himself, despite my circumstances, I feel an overwhelming gratitude. Jesus has been enduring my wounds with me since our first step. When I realize I'm not alone in my sufferings, my cross doesn't seem so unbearable anymore.

I cry out in pain as a knife tears through the thick rope fibers that still dig deeply into my raw wrists. The ropes quickly drop to the ground but it takes a moment for the heavy wooden beam to follow. When it does, it rips off multiple layers of sticky, crusty skin and a cry erupts from my mouth.

But the simultaneous relief that I feel is inexplicable. Once my cross falls to the ground, the burden no longer on my shoulders, I can take a full breath for the first time in what feels like years. Exhausted, lungs full, I fall face down into the mud. I'm so disoriented that I hardly hear the guards carrying over more wooden beams, nailing them together.

Our means of execution.

Knowing the end is near, I begin giving into the pull of darkness. I hardly hear the soldiers yelling at us to climb onto our formed crosses. I barely feel the whips of glass and leather across my bare chest. I don't even know if the crowds are yelling anymore. But when I see Jesus climb onto His cross and lean into it, I do the same.

The looming darkness is so close to overtaking me when I hear Jesus cry out.

My eyes shoot open and what I see almost takes the life out of me. I knew this was coming, but I never actually imagined it happening. Two soldiers kneel on Jesus' chest while another stretches out His arm. A fourth man kneels in the mud. In one hand he holds a thick, sharpened iron nail, which hovers over Jesus' wrist. The other hand holds a wooden mallet, drawn high in the air, ready to strike.

They're going to nail Him to His cross.

My whole body trembles and my breathing shallows. I feel as though I'm already dying of the asphyxiation to come.

Then they're going to nail me to mine.

Jesus' cry makes me go completely still. Tears spill out of my tightly closed eyes and I clench my teeth. But nothing can save me from the sound of metal tearing His sacred flesh, pounding through thick, resistant bones. As the soldiers force the nails into Jesus' body, I cry out in unison with Him. His pain is my pain. I thought the strikes of the hammer would sound like rumbles of thunder – I wish I didn't know it has its own distinct bone-shattering sound.

It takes five swings for each nail.

I lay shivering, shaking, bawling. My breathing shallows as I anticipate the pain to come. Eyes still closed, my body thrashes, desperately trying to escape. And then I feel a still, small invitation tug on my heart.

Look to Me for comfort.

I open my eyes and look to the lacerated Man beside me. Our eyes meet and everything stands still, including my body. As I behold the face of my Messiah, He looks right at me. His labored breathing quickens, He's struggling to say something. I lean closer. His whisper sounds like a gentle breeze.

"Beloved... you are... not alone."

When the sudden pain rips through my wrist, my eyes grow wide but they never leave His. With each pound of the hammer, my whole being lurches. I see my immense pain mirrored in His eyes. My pain is His pain. The tears rolling down His cheeks mirror mine. I'm not alone. Not during the first five blows or the next. Not when they stack my trembling feet, one atop the other, and penetrate bone after bone after bone.

Thwack, thwack, thwack, thwack, thwack.

Through it all, Jesus is here. His eyes on me, my eyes on Him.

After my brother is nailed to his cross, the guards raise our crosses and we hang in the fullest form of humiliation. My brother, Jesus, and me. I can't tell if I'm shaking because of the pain or the thunder causing the earth to rumble beneath us. Bodies maimed, wrists and feet nailed, we're utterly drained. This is where we'll suffocate. This is where we'll die.

This is our end.

Gravity pulls at my decaying body, instantly choking me. I watch Jesus redistribute His weight, pushing up on His scourged feet to take a breath before letting gravity take over again. When I try to do the same, pain shoots throughout my entire body, the nails in my flesh feel like they're on fire. But at least for a moment I can breathe. When I can't handle the pain any longer, I let gravity take over again. I feel immediate relief from the pain but start choking instantly. The cycle continues for what feels like an eternity. *It hurts to exist.*

I look down at the soldiers below us and they seem so small. Laughing, they rip apart a purple tunic, rolling dice for it. It reminds me that I'm nearly naked. Looking at my pale, bloodied body, I hardly recognize it. Looking over at my brother, I hardly recognize him, either.

My brother is silent, his body still. My heart races. *Is he already dead?* I don't care that I might pass out, I push up on my feet as quickly as I can. Gulping in air I cry out.

"Brother!"

His body moves, I hope it's not just the wind. Finally he lulls his head toward me. Eyes hardly open, he looks exhausted. For his sake I hope he passes soon, but I feel there's still more that needs to be said between us before we're separated by eternal darkness. I watch as he fights to breathe, to hold onto life, desperately gasping for air. His lungs have probably already filled with fluid. For the first time in my life I want to protect him. Another part of me wants to put my head down, to turn away, to not watch. But he's my brother and I promised my mother I would stay with him until the end. *I'm glad you made me promise, Mama.*

My brother desperately pushes up on his feet, gathering what will likely be his last breath. Looking toward me I can tell he's trying to say something. I strain my head so he can use as little energy as possible. He has to shout through the downpour of rain.

"I'm sorry... little brother..." It's the weakest shout I've ever heard. As he sucks in more air, I can audibly hear his lungs collapsing. His chest isn't moving up and down like it's supposed to, the air is going nowhere. I want to tell him to stop, to save his breath, but I need to know what he wants to say. He continues.

"I... made you suffer... I should've... looked out... for you..."

I feel a sob building in my own collapsing chest.

"The ruby..." he goes on, "I saw it... and thought... Mama would... love it... I stole because... I missed her..."

Are the sobs I hear leaving my throat or his? This is simultaneously the most excruciating and healing moment of our lives. I stifle my groans as he continues.

"Death stole... Mama from us... so I stole back... to feel... in control... I'm truly sorry. little brother... thank you... for staying with me... to the end..."

I speak the only words I can form, "Mama would... forgive you... and so... do I..."

I mourn the fact that I don't have the breath to express the totality of my understanding and forgiveness to him.

My brother pushes up, gasping for more air and then speaks directly to Jesus, "If You're... really God... save us!"

I can hear the anger in his voice, but I know he truly desires to be liberated. Jesus turns His head away from me, toward my brother. Their exchange is inaudible over the pounding rain and the suddenly riled crowd. I'll never know the words they're speaking. When they're done, my big brother looks at me one last time. His eyes are soft again. He lifts his face towards the sky and closes his eyes. He breathes his last and his head falls. He's gone.

I cry at the loss of my brother, a graver pain than any laceration I bear.

The crowds below must've heard my brother's final plea for help. They start yelling similar phrases at Jesus, but their words drip with accusation and mockery. "If You're really God, why don't You come down from Your cross?"

I look to Jesus and hear His response in the form of a pained whisper, "Forgive them... Father... for they know not... what they do..."

Even in His tortuous suffering, our Savior forgives. I desire this forgiveness that He offers. But panic begins to fill my chest as a realization sinks in. *I don't have the breath in my lungs to confess all of my wrongs.* But then I look into His eyes and I'm filled with peace.

In true contrition I speak the only words I can muster.

"I'm... sorry..."

Looking at Jesus, I know it's enough. He knows all and He forgives me.

At this moment I'm convinced that He would do all of this, over and over again just for me. So that I'd never be alone, so that I could receive His forgiveness, so that I could personally know His love.

What a beautiful gift to receive in my final hour. But there's still one more thing I deeply desire. *I don't want to be forgotten.* My mother and my brother are dead. The only other person who cares about me and knows me hangs beside me. I remember my mother talking about the Messiah's Kingdom. Maybe while I'm in the eternal darkness of death, He can remember me there.

"Jesus..." I say, between ragged breaths. "Will You... remember me... when You come... into... Your Kingdom?"

Jesus looks right at me and gasps back, "Brother... I say to you... today you will... be *with* Me... in Paradise..."

Under His gaze, the magnificent truth starts to sink in. *To simply remember me is not enough for Him. Jesus wants to spend eternity with me.* I'm overwhelmed by the goodness of my Messiah. Through His love I'm no longer abandoned. I'm no longer an orphan. I'm no longer a robber.

I'm Redeemed. *And today I'll be with Him in Paradise.*

I start to go in and out of consciousness. I'm in a delirium for what feels like hours. But whenever I become aware, I slowly look over to Jesus. He's always looking back at me.

When it is finished, a ray of light pierces through the dark clouds and I hear Jesus cry out in a loud voice toward the sky, "Father, into Your hands I commend My Spirit!" As He breathes His last, His head falls and the ground begins to shake fiercely. It's as if a veil between death and life is being torn from the top down.

A sharp pain shoots through my knees as a soldier breaks them and lowers me to the ground. Looking up, I see the two lifeless bodies of my brothers hanging above me, but I know this isn't the end. It's only the beginning.

The way of the cross changed my life. And the weight of my cross, which once seemed unbearable, was the exact means that drew me close to Jesus. When I was nailed to it, in the very grips of death, He healed me. My cross was my greatest gift.

Because of Jesus, death is no longer eternal darkness but eternal life.

As I feel this new life approaching, I'm deeply at peace. It's as if I'm wrapped in my mother's arms once again. I welcome my end, speaking the words I learned from my Messiah.

"Father, into Your hands I commend my spirit."

Taking a final breath, I close my eyes to darkness and open them to glory.

THE DEFILED TOMB

John 20:1-18; John 8:1-11

"Where are You, my Lord?!" I cry out into the darkness.

Tears stream down my cheeks and my guttural wails echo off the walls of the empty tomb before me. This resting place of our Lord has been defiled, ransacked, emptied.

Everything is empty now.

Even the flowers I'd brought Him have lost their color. Blackness blankets the whole earth. It's the watch before dawn, the darkest hour of the night. I stare at the tomb stone that was supposed to keep Jesus safe, as safe as a dead body can be. A stone so heavy it could crush a man. Though, seeing it beside the opening of the tomb, it feels like it's crushing me.

Suddenly another wave of harsh, vivid memories from the past days rip through my mind...

The torture, the mocking, the stripping, the scourging. His gushing blood, His tears, His shoulder roughly torn from its socket.

The heavy, splintered wood thrown across His wounded back. The jagged crown clinging to His skull.

The wrought-iron nails, the dull hammer.

The torn garments, His nakedness.

The sounds of tearing flesh.

I saw more than any human being should ever have to see. I watched my best friend as He was murdered, and I was unprotected from a single detail of the gruesome act. I thought I'd learned what trauma was in Magdala, but I had no idea.

I don't regret staying close to Jesus in His suffering but it came with a price. His groans of pain are still so close, as if He is in this garden with me. I can't escape the haunting wail that strained from His collapsing lungs as they drove the thickest nail into the resistant bones of His feet, one atop the other. The smell of blood had been thick in the air. I can almost taste it now, as if I'm still at the base of the cross.

I'd accompanied Jesus' mother along the way of the cross, I'd held her against my chest as they drove a rusty spear into the flesh of His heart that was no longer beating. A seemingly unnecessary torture to His breathless body and to her sorrowful heart. I can still feel her body shaking in mine. Then we went to the tomb where they laid her little boy, now just torn flesh, on a stone slab. I'd almost fainted in the tomb but I'd grabbed the slab to steady myself.

The stone had been cold, just like His body.

Because He's dead. He's gone and I'm here, though I feel dead, too.

I weep.

Too tired to yell anymore, I pound the cold, hard ground that I kneel on. It's cracked, parched, lifeless, just like the rest of us.

After His burial we'd gone back to His mother's house. Even though I was exhausted, I couldn't sleep. Although He was dead, I just wanted

The Defiled Tomb

to be close to Him. On the second night, I took a lantern and some of Jesus' favorite flowers from His mother's garden. All of the flowers were in full bloom except for one tight bud that refused to burst forth. I almost left it behind, but Jesus always loved things with the potential to grow.

Everything reminds me of Him... and that He no longer has breath. I'd wept along the way to the burial garden. And that's when I came upon His opened tomb.

Robbed. Empty. Defiled.

The flowers fell from my hand. I was in shock – I couldn't move. Maybe there was a misunderstanding. I ran to the disciples to see if they'd know why. I pounded on the door, waking them. Their hair was tousled, eyes fearful and confused. Peter, John, and I took off running. We approached the tomb. Peter went in first, unknowingly stepping on the flowers I'd dropped. John followed. It was still empty. They had no explanation. Wailing, we fell to our knees. Even in death He's being ripped away from us.

Who's going to believe us? How are we going to find Him? And who's going to tell His mother?

Peter and John went back to the house. When they left I laid down just outside the tomb next to His favorite blossoms, now trampled, now completely crushed. Just like me.

I haven't moved from this spot.

I have no concept of time. I don't know how long I've been here or if I've drifted into the relief of rest. It feels like I've been asleep for days, trapped in a merciless nightmare. But I know this pain is far too agonizing to be a dream. I hope I've been lying here for many days, because that means fewer days I have to spend without Him.

Face in the dirt, I lay before Jesus' tomb. Raw, exhausted, numb. The weight of its vacancy is crushing. Its hollow mouth breathes a hot breath of despair over me, reminding me that He's no longer here, *that I'm utterly alone.*

I strain to look at the crushed flowers I'd picked for Jesus, now just inches away from my face. My only companion. I try to reach for them, but my arm is too heavy and falls to the dusty ground.

It doesn't matter, they're as good as dead anyway.

I inhale dust. Coughing, my mind flashes back to the day I met Jesus. I'd been lying in the dust then, too. Nearly naked, covered only by a bed sheet, I'd been shoved to the ground, encircled by bantering men. I was at the mercy of the Pharisees. As tears and paint streamed down my face, they laughed as two men strained to pick up a large stone together.

Then the crowds had suddenly hushed. A pair of feet approached me and I cowered, ready for the first blow. But it didn't come. I remember Jesus' strong fingers, carefully drawing in the dirt. I'll never forget the power in what He wrote. Then rocks fell to the ground with heavy thuds, dust filled the air. Everyone walked away – everyone except for Jesus.

I'll never forget the words He spoke to me then, after I'd just been caught in adultery, an act stained with utter shame.

"Neither do I condemn you, beloved."

A single tear rolls down my cheek, I would give anything to hear Him say these words to me again. Painful memories from my life

The Defiled Tomb

before I met Jesus flood my mind. I close my eyes tightly, trying in vain to escape the defiling images I'd long tried to forget. The empty tomb taunts me. *In the darkness of the night, Jesus isn't here to defend you anymore. It'll go back to being like before He was ever in your life.* I shudder at this realization.

I suddenly hear footsteps approaching and my heart quickens. A smile spreads deeply across my face but it disappears as quickly as it came. For a moment I thought maybe it was Jesus coming to console me. For a moment I'd forgotten He's dead.

The figure draws nearer. It's still pitch black. I'm too tired to be scared of who it could be.

I hold up my lantern to see a pair of scarred feet approaching me. Looking up in the dim light I take in a face that seems familiar, but I don't know Him. Yet I've seen those eyes before... Is He one of the people I saw Jesus heal during the three years of ministry? Or maybe He's one of the many disciples who traveled with us? I can't remember, but by His work tunic, I think He must be the Gardener.

Suddenly my heart begins to race again, eyes growing wide. Maybe He knows where Jesus' body is! I stumble to my feet, speaking almost too quickly to make sense.

"Gardener," I fumble, "where have You carried my Lord's body? Please tell me so I can–"

My words stop abruptly when I notice the distinct scar on His arm.

The hair on my neck stands straight up and fear pulses through my entire body. I begin to shake. My right hand lifts my sleeve to reveal a scar on my own arm, which now burns with pain. The Gardener's mark is smooth and light, but otherwise they look identical. My finger traces the rough etching on my skin. I look at it, raised and discolored, and feel disgusted with myself. I think I might throw up.

My heartbeat quickens and I sweat despite the cool of the night. I hadn't thought of this scar and the petrifying circumstances that caused it since long before I met Jesus. Partly because I'd wanted to leave my past behind me and start a new life in following Jesus. But the real reason was because I knew I wasn't physically capable of reliving that trauma, so I'd simply blocked out the memory.

But it's too late now. The memory is back in full. Shame and fear attack me like a raging lion and panic seizes my whole being. My throat tightens as the intrusive sounds and images of that excruciating memory scourge me without mercy. I can barely manage to push them away for a single second before they come rushing upon me again. My body convulses with each assault. It will only be a matter of seconds until the memory completely takes over. I can't hold it off much longer and I certainly can't be in the presence of the Gardener when it happens.

My vision begins to tunnel and my breathing shallows. I can't catch my breath. It's like there's an enemy hovering over me. I can't see it but it's there, strangling me. I stumble backwards and the Gardener reaches out His arm to help me. But all I see is His scar – or is it mine – thrusted at me.

"No, stop!" I shout, instinctively. And I immediately regret it. All I want is to be helped! But I can't let anyone see me like this, so out of control. I need to get away, *now*.

I turn in panic, tripping over my mourning shawl and hitting the hard ground. I cry out, feeling a biting pain in my knee, which bore the brunt of the fall. I get up quickly, looking around frantically, limping to the only place that I know to hide.

The darkness of the empty tomb.

I grope in the pitch blackness, smashing my injured knee, now throbbing, on the stone burial slab. I'd forgotten the lantern. I crawl onto the cold rock and curl up into a ball. Any bit of control over these attacking flashbacks is lost the moment I realize that I'm laying on the same stone where Jesus' dead body was laid only days ago.

Jesus is gone.

I can't stifle the flashbacks any longer. I lay on the burial stone and I'm overtaken. Like a helpless baby left screaming, alone, I plead for help in vain. I cover my mouth firmly with both hands, trying to stifle my shrieks so that the Gardener won't hear me. Eyes shut tightly, the full of the memory floods my being.

The vicious man in Magdala. His freshly sharpened knife at my throat, threatening to kill. His degrading words, disgustingly whispered in my ear. The deep shame that took root, knowing his words were true. His yells, my screaming, the pain. The moment he realized he couldn't use me anymore if I was dead and his lasting decision to leave a permanent mark on my body instead, ensuring that I'd never forget the power he holds over me.

I wince, my tears burn as I remember what came next. *His sharp knife cutting into the skin on my arm as he carved his initials, branding me forever.* My disfigured scar pulsates with stabbing pains, like it's being ripped open all over again. The wound feels fresh. My whole being screams!

More images of Magdala join the assault...

The torture, the mocking, the abuse.

The blood, the tears, my hair being roughly torn out.

The heavy, splintering burden of shame thrown across my shoulders, constantly clinging to me.

The jewelry that felt like shackles, the dull face paint.

The torn garments, my nakedness.

The sounds of tearing flesh.

Voices in the darkness join the bombarding images, reminding me of my disgusting sins. *You're not worthy of respect, forgiveness, or love. Your stains are your identity.*

Maybe they're right.

Jesus had loved me but He never saw my scar, which was always covered by my sleeve. I feel my face grow warm. I never told Him what happened, what I'd done before the day He wrote in the sand. *Did He think that was the only time I'd been impure?* Maybe if He'd known I'd been branded, if He'd known what I'd done before He saved me... He would've treated me like the whore that I am.

The thought stings like a slap in the face.

The voices in the darkness are overwhelming, I don't know what's true anymore. I'm so anxious I can't stay still any longer. I get off of the stone and walk to the opening of the tomb. Looking into the darkness, I try to clear my head. I try to remember what Jesus' love was like before He was slaughtered.

I'm suddenly overwhelmed by an unexpected ache, a deep grief that I'll never be able to share my past with Jesus. As terrifying as it would've been, I'll never be able to ask Him to heal me. I'll never know for sure if He would have condemned me, knowing me fully. But it's too late. He's gone. I hold my face in my hands, overwhelmed by the crushing weight of this reality.

My Healer is dead and I'll never be known. My disfigured scar aches. I ache.

Then I'm hit with another grave heaviness. *If I die right now, no one else will know about what that man in Magdala did to me. What all of those men did to me. No one else will know my deep, gut-wrenching sufferings. I'll be alone in them forever.* The thought nearly breaks me.

The isolation in this defiled tomb is suffocating. I wish someone were here to listen. I don't want to be alone in my sufferings anymore. I need someone to know... anyone...

I lift my head to see a figure standing just outside of the tomb. It's the Gardener. He must've stayed to make sure I was okay, keeping His distance out of respect for my privacy. We lock eyes. My heart lifts the smallest bit and for the first time since Jesus' death, I feel less alone.

The Gardener has a similar scar and maybe He'll understand my pain. I'm glad He didn't leave.

He nods His head silently, asking my permission to enter. I smile, tiredly, welcoming Him into the tomb. He brings light with Him as He enters. He seems to carry peace with Him just as easily as He carries the lantern and trampled flowers that are in His hands. His presence doesn't feel intrusive.

I sit down on the stone slab and He joins me. I feel a firm yet gentle stirring in my heart.

Lift up your sleeve. Show Him your scar. Share your story with this Gardener.

My heart begins to race again but I take a deep breath. I don't want to miss another opportunity to let someone in. I let out a breath and dare to look at His scar. It's the exact same shape as mine, but His is different. Smooth, light, somehow even beautiful.

I close my eyes and take another deep breath before lifting my sleeve, revealing my own scar to Him. I keep my eyes tightly closed, unable to look at it myself. Unable to look at the Gardener.

After only a few moments I hear Him take a few short breaths. I open my eyes to see that His are filled with tears. He looks at my disfigured scar for a long time, as if He's listening to me tell its story without me saying any words. I'd expected to see disgust across His face, but instead I see deep empathy. When He's tenderly taken in my wound and its story in full, He nods in understanding.

I look at His scar again. *I wonder who branded Him?*

He looks at His own arm then back to my eyes, as if offering His scar to me. I reach out my trembling hand, tracing His scar with my finger, then tracing my own. As I do, a small seed of empathy takes root in my heart for the man who branded me. I wonder how I could feel any type of ache for a man who hurt me so severely and yet I do. *What did he go through that made him so aggressive as to need to feel power over me?*

In bravery, I decide to look at my scar and fully acknowledge what I've been through because of it. Dark and raised, it barely aches anymore after this encounter. For the first time since the knife broke my skin,

The Defiled Tomb

I don't have the urge to turn away from my wound. It scares me a little less now. I think it's because I'm no longer alone in it. Someone else knows of my suffering. The scar and its memories have lost their power over me.

I start to breathe more easily when another painful and long-forgotten memory forces itself upon me. Instinctively, I want to shove it down, to pretend it never happened. But I don't. Instead, I hold my palms out to the Gardener. The many scars sprinkled across my hands look like a field of wildflowers from a bird's-eye-view. They glow in the light of the lantern.

My skin begins to burn.

Every part of me wants to pull my hands away, to hide them in the surrounding darkness like I've done for so many years. But I know that will only lead to further pain. So I keep my hands wide open to Him, and I let the memory rush upon me.

The passerby roughly shoving me to the ground. My bleeding palms, filled with gravel. The harsh kick to my ribs, the distinct snap of one of them. The spreading pain, my shallowed breathing. The sharp sound of spit leaving his mouth, and the stinging warmth it brought when it landed in my eye. The degrading words he'd yelled loud enough to turn heads.

"You're the stain of the village!"

He'd been right... I don't know if the man's words stung worse then or now. Tears burn the corners of my eyes. As the Gardener looks at my scarred hands, I keep my face down in shame.

The Gardener gently holds my palms and pulls them towards Himself. I stare at the ugly, jagged little scars and I see a tear fall onto them.

Sacred Wounds

It's not mine. Emotion is rolling down the Gardener's cheeks as He acknowledges each little wound. Not one is overlooked. This Man takes in the story of these scars and, looking at His face, it's as if He knows my pain personally.

He looks at me through wet eyes and places His hands on top of mine. His palms are covered in similar scars. I feel myself get choked up and I'm moved to weeping. My empathy deepens and overwhelming gratitude takes root.

Who is this Gardener?

Looking into His eyes, I notice a series of light scars covering the right side of His face. Without a thought, I lift my hand to feel the matching ones that decorate my own cheek. I close my eyes and remember. It's excruciating. My scars feel like they're on fire as the memory comes.

The day my father disowned me.

He was a wealthy man, well renowned by the religious elders and prestigious men of the town. Though I was treated like his most prized possession in public, I was his slave behind closed doors. I never resisted his control until that day. He married me off to a notoriously abusive man in exchange for luxurious, sizable rubies. One for each of his fingers. When I refused, I was met with the back of his hand and the jewelry that adorned it. The pure gems cut deeply into my cheek, breaking my nose along the way.

"*Now what man will marry you with a face like that? Get out of my sight, you worthless worm. I never want to see you again!*" My father's words still ring in my ears.

The Defiled Tomb

The Gardener silently listens as I relive the memory. We both shed tears, eyes heavy with pain. The Gardener places His hand on my scarred cheek, and I place mine on His. Without hesitation I allow Him, the only person since that day, to approach my deeply personal wounds. His touch is a balm to my pain.

The suffering isn't gone, but we're no longer alone in it.

Moving my hand, I touch His temple, realizing that His entire forehead is covered in these smooth, light scars. The marks around His brows and the edges of His scalp are distinct. They were clearly caused by extremely deep gashes. I don't know what happened to this Gardener, but He's undoubtedly experienced immense torture. My heart hurts for Him.

One by one, I take in all of these scars around His face. One in particular catches my eye. It's just below His brow and it looks like something sharp was dug deeply into His tender skin. I don't physically carry this wound but I recognize it. I carry it on my mind.

It's the agonizing mental torture, the constant nagging questions about my identity and my worth. *Who am I? Will I ever be truly known? Am I as worthless as they say that I am?* These are the questions that have long gnawed at me, day after day, man after man. My head constantly throbs from this thorn in my forehead.

The questions tumble freshly in my mind, and the voices of darkness begin to speak again. *You're a whore, that's who you are. No man will ever want to marry you now, let alone truly know you. You're the stain of the village, remember? Beyond repair. Utterly worthless.*

I feel the Gardener's hand on my chin. He tilts my face up so that I'm looking into His eyes and the voices stop. They are silenced immediately. He cups my face and draws closer, kissing me right on the forehead where His wound – and mine – are carried, just below my brow. The throbbing stills and even though I still don't know the answer to these questions, I feel a deep peace. Like maybe this Man has different answers. I see a few strands of light dancing along the upper wall of the tomb. It's growing lighter and we no longer need the lantern. Dawn is almost here.

Suddenly, I feel something warm sliding down my leg. Dark red blood soaks my linen dress, which now sticks to my knee. Lifting it, I see a shallow gash in my skin. It must be from when I tripped. The Gardener tears a piece of material from His work tunic and wraps it gently, yet firmly. The bleeding slows. One final wound tended by the Gardener.

Gratitude seeps deeply into the newly tilled soil of my heart. I smile, slightly. Amidst the devastation of losing Jesus, this encounter has consoled me deeply. Morning light freely streams into the tomb now and I place my hand on the stone slab one last time. Taking a deep breath I walk to the opening of the tomb, scanning the garden for Jesus' body in the new light. I start forming a plan of action in my head. When I go back to the other disciples we can form a search party. Then we'll find Jesus and finally lay Him to rest.

With my face still forward, I ask, "Gardener, did You move My Lord's body? If You did, I know You must have had a good reason. Please tell me where You laid Him so I can go to Him."

I turn toward the Gardener to hear His reply. He's smiling at me, tenderly.

"Mary!"

When Jesus says my name I recognize His voice immediately! The voice that has always spoken my name with tenderness and love. The voice that didn't condemn me then and doesn't condemn me now. How did I not see it all along? His smile. His eyes. His gentle gaze. I burst into tears and run into Jesus' arms, sinking into His comforting embrace. He holds my shaking body. After all that I've been through these past three days, He knows I need to be held.

Soon my tears slow. I step back, taking all of Him in. I'm overwhelmed with deep joy as I bask in the goodness of my Gardener. I can't believe He's here! I can't believe He's alive again! In complete awe I laugh and He joins in.

Like a little child, I ask all of my questions at once until I run out of breath. "What happened? Where did You go? Wait, did someone take Your body? How are You here?" Before He has a chance to answer I throw my arms around Him again. I can't help it! I listen in anticipation for what He's going to tell me. He smiles deeply at me, like a loving father looking at his precious little girl.

"I went to see My Father and open the gates of Heaven. I carried all of the wounds of humanity with Me and I have now come back to bring new life to all. See, beloved, I am making all things new!"

As I process His words, I'm drawn once again to all of His scars. In the darkness of night, I'd only seen the few that resemble my own. But now that the tomb has brightened, I see the tens of thousands that cover His body. Some are deep and wide, others small and shallow, all of them are stunning. No wonder He looks so different.

And yet, I recognize them all. I'd seen Jesus' dead, bleeding body before it was wrapped in the burial cloths. In that moment, He was simply open flesh. Now, all of those gaping wounds have been healed.

Sacred Wounds

They've become beautiful, gloriously redeemed. It's breathtaking. I never knew scars could be so beautiful.

I look again to the scars He carries that are so similar to my own. And then it hits me. *These don't just look like my wounds – they are my wounds. Jesus carried them to Heaven with Him and now they're redeemed. My scars have been reclaimed by Him.* Seeing my glorified scars on Jesus, I feel a deep sense of promise. One day my scars will look like that, too. All of my deepest hurts and fears will be brought from glory to glory. I look at Jesus in awe.

All along I thought my wounds would be the thing to keep me from Heaven, but they were the first part of me there.

Jesus continues, "Thank you, My beloved one, for sharing your wounds with Me in the tomb. I know the immense pain they carry and the incredible courage it took for you to be vulnerable with Me. You have done well and I am proud of you. I know you desire full healing, and you will receive it in My perfect timing..."

His voice trails off and He smiles, as though He's looking at what I'll become in my full glory. "Your full healing will come, Mary. But for now, come and rest, My brave little one." I sink into Jesus, relieved that I don't need to worry. We watch the sun burst over the horizon from inside the tomb, together. My Gardener is here and He'll tend to my healing.

Deeply content, I look toward the opening of the tomb, excited for what Jesus has in store. He gently gathers my hands in His. I turn to see the love in His eyes that I've seen so many times before.

He still has more to give.

"You have shown Me your wounds and I would like to show you one of Mine."

The Defiled Tomb

Honor pours over me like blessed oil. Outside of His inner circle, He rarely reveals His full nature. *This wound is very personal to Him, and He's inviting me in.* I know immediately that I'm approaching Holy Ground. My hands tremble in anticipation and fear of my Lord. In utter humility, I receive.

Jesus reaches toward the tear in His tunic. Pulling the pieces of linen apart He reveals the deepest wound I've ever seen and I gasp. The massive gash in His strong abdomen looks like a deep canyon. I'm captivated. It's like nothing I've ever seen before. His side has been opened to reveal something deeper.

Bright morning light floods the tomb and now I can see without hindrance. I watch as Jesus gently pulls back the pieces of flesh to reveal His Heart. I look more closely into His body and see His pulsing flesh.

Human. Pierced. Divine. Beating. It's extraordinary.

I see a drop of deep red blood seep from the opening where His Heart is pierced and in that moment my identity and worth are made clear. The throbbing questions of who I am are finally answered by Jesus.

I'm known. I'm worthy. I'm His.

My eyes move from His Sacred Heart to His gentle gaze. We look at one another and the weight of what we've shared, the unfathomable beauty of what has taken place, sinks in. Hope wells within my heart, like a flower bursting in springtime. I look once more at the scar on my arm, the one that used to control me. I smile, now knowing what it shall become. *Glorious, like Him.*

Morning light dances across the full walls of the tomb. The darkness is gone. I watch Jesus reach toward the trampled flowers I brought

Him, still lying on the stone slab. He plucks something from the bunch. My eyes widen when I see it's a perfect flower in full bloom, bursting with new life. But I don't understand. How could any of the flowers have survived?

And then I realize it must've been the tight little bud, the one that seemingly refused to grow. The one I almost threw out. *The one that just needed time to bloom.*

Smiling, Jesus places the fragrant flower behind my ear. Hand-in-hand, my Gardener and I walk out of the empty tomb and into the light of a new morning.

THE GARDEN

"Dry bones, hear the word of the LORD! Thus says the Lord GOD to these bones: Listen! I will make breath enter you so you may come to life."

– *Ezekiel 37:4-5* –

HOLY GROUND

All I see is abundance.

New life blooms forth in every direction. The sweet-smelling greenery that surrounds me is splashed with the most brilliant of colors. I feel like I'm immersed in the painting of a masterful Artist as I take in the grandeur. It's breathtaking. I've never been here before, I would've remembered the vibrant colors and dripping fragrances, but it somehow feels familiar.

Dressed in white, I make my way to the center of this garden and sit below a large, strong oak tree. Its leaves sway in the breeze and its branches are filled with little blue birds. Its large roots sink into the soft soil and they drink deeply from a nearby river rushing with fresh water. The variety of sounds from nature and the creatures that fill it make a symphony. Leaning back against the firm trunk, I pluck a small, plump fig from one of the many blooming vines. My mouth bursts with sweetness as I enjoy the harvest. Looking up into the tree above me I smile deeply as I watch the little birds hop from branch to branch freely.

I feel free, too.

I'm overjoyed when I see the One who invited me here walking toward me, His bare feet pressing into the soil of the land. He sits beside me and smiles, delighting over me as I take in the expanse of beauty that seems to go on forever. When He speaks, I'm comforted by His familiar voice.

"Do you recognize this place, beloved?"

As I study the landscape, the hill far off to the left, and the crevice of grassy earth just a few feet away, I suddenly recognize the curves and divots. My eyes fill with tears. It looks so different now.

My valley of dry bones, my once-desolate land.

Warm tears spill over as I take in what used to be my hopeless dwelling place. This land where I once knew my brokenness most intimately has become the very place where I am most intimately known. This scene that once terrified me is now a source of tremendous joy. This valley that was once a place of death has become a garden of new life.

And Jesus did all of this *for me*. In His goodness He restored the land of my aching heart.

I watch as Jesus picks a blooming flower. Placing it behind my ear, He speaks. "I am so proud of you for entering your valley. All along I could not wait to gift you this garden! It is My great joy to restore the hearts of My children and bestow good things upon them. Many are afraid to begin, but when surrendered to Me, anything can be turned into beauty in ways unimaginable. No bone is too dry, no valley too vast for My Love. *The greater the valley, the more glorious the garden!* Thank you, beloved, for being a witness to My Heart of Mercy."

With His staff in hand and His face beaming, Jesus continues, "And this is just the beginning! Where do you want to go first, My friend?"

I'm overwhelmed with a gratitude for my Father that sinks in like new roots. Looking around in awe and excitement I wonder at the possibilities. We could climb the tree and experience the expanse of the garden from high above or we could run through the tall grass with our arms outstretched or we could walk barefoot in the creek and skip rocks. My heart almost bursts knowing that we get to explore it all together. What a glorious adventure!

Without even thinking, I run into the open field of wildflowers. Throwing my arms out to my sides and looking toward the sky, I laugh. I feel Jesus grab my hands and we dance in the garden together, smiling and breathless.

As we spin, the words He once spoke to me echo throughout the newly blooming canyons of my heart, "I have done this for you so that My joy may be in you, and your joy may be complete."

"I have spoken; I will do it."

– *Ezekiel 37:14* –

NOTES

Scripture and other resources that served as inspiration

Prologue
- "Rend your hearts, not your garments." Joel 2:13
- "God said: Do not come near! Remove your sandals from your feet, for the place where you stand is holy ground." Exodus 3:5
- "God will not be outdone in generosity." St. Ignatius of Loyola

Desolate Land
- "He made me walk among them in every direction. So many lay on the surface of the valley! How dry they were!" Ezekiel 37:2
- "I have told you this so that my joy may be in you and your joy may be complete." John 15:11

The Barren Fig Tree
- "... he restores my soul." Psalm 23:3
- "Then Jesus said, 'Neither do I condemn you.'" John 8:11
- "God is love..." 1 John 4:16
- "One thing I do know is that I was blind and now I see." John 9:25
- Pope Francis' call for evangelists to take on the "smell of sheep," *Evangelii Gaudium*, #24

The Red-Stained Linen
- "God is love..." 1 John 4:16

- "...but the LORD was not in the wind... the LORD was not in the earthquake... the LORD was not in the fire; after the fire, a light silent sound." 1 Kings 19:12
- "...and hope does not disappoint..." Romans 5:5
- "It is finished." John 19:30
- "And Jesus wept." John 11:35
- "What I am doing, you do not understand now, but you will understand later." John 13:7
- "...David and all the house of Israel danced before the LORD with all their might..." 2 Samuel 6:5
- "With age-old love have I loved you." Jeremiah 31:3
- "Be utterly amazed! For a work is being done in your days that you would not believe, were it told." Habakkuk 1:5
- C.S. Lewis' description of Aslan and Shasta's walk in the dark, *The Horse and His Boy*

The Binding Burial Cloths

- "The whole head is sick, the whole heart is faint. From the sole of the foot to the head there is no sound spot on it." Isaiah 1:6
- "And behold, I am with you always, until the end of the age." Matthew 28:20
- "God said: Do not come near! Remove your sandals from your feet, for the place where you stand is holy ground." Exodus 3:5
- "...the King of kings and Lord of lords." 1 Timothy 6:15
- "You formed my inmost being..." Psalm 139:13
- "Be not afraid!" Pope St. John Paul II
- St. Francis of Assisi's encounter with Jesus disguised as a leper
- "You are magnificent" - *The Butterfly Circus*, short film

Notes

The Unbreachable Door

- "As Moses came down from Mount Sinai with the two tablets of the covenant in his hands... the skin of his face had become radiant..." Exodus 34:29
- "I do believe, help my unbelief!" Mark 9:24
- "Where, O death, is your victory? Where, O death, is your sting?" 1 Corinthians 15:55
- "Amen, I say to you, if you have faith the size of a mustard seed, you will say to this mountain, 'Move from here to there,' and it will move." Matthew 17:20
- "In my deepest wound I saw your glory, and it dazzled me." St. Augustine

The Broken Staff

- "I have told you this so that my joy may be in you and your joy may be complete." John 15:11
- "For my thoughts are not your thoughts, nor are your ways my ways..." Isaiah 55:8
- "God said: Do not come near! Remove your sandals from your feet, for the place where you stand is holy ground." Exodus 3:5
- "Then Jesus said, 'Neither do I condemn you.'" John 8:11
- "...perhaps it was for a time like this that you became queen?" Esther 4:14
- "For every boot that tramped in battle, every cloak rolled in blood, will be burned as fuel for fire." Isaiah 9:4
- The detail that the only two charcoal fires in Scripture are in John 18:18 and John 21:9, source unknown
- "The night my best friend in the world needed me, I denied even knowing him." Fr. Mike Schmitz, *Bible in a Year* podcast

The Shattered Alabaster

- "...but the LORD was not in the wind... the LORD was not in the earthquake... the LORD was not in the fire; after the fire, a light silent sound." 1 Kings 19:12
- "The LORD, your God... will rejoice over you with gladness... will sing joyfully because of you, as on festival days." Zephaniah 3:17
- "...and the sheep hear his voice, as he calls his own sheep by name and leads them out... and the sheep follow him, because they recognize his voice." John 10:3-4
- "How beautiful is your love, my sister, my bride." Song of Songs 4:10
- "Being unwanted, unloved, uncared for, forgotten by everybody, I think that is a much greater hunger, a much greater poverty than the person who has nothing to eat." St. Mother Teresa of Calcutta
- "Dear Jesus, help me to spread Your fragrance everywhere I go. Flood my soul with Your spirit and life." St. Mother Teresa of Calcutta

The Unbearable Cross

- "God is love..." 1 John 4:16
- "...but the LORD was not in the wind... the LORD was not in the earthquake... the LORD was not in the fire; after the fire, a light silent sound." 1 Kings 19:12
- "...the King of kings and Lord of lords." 1 Timothy 6:15
- "But I am a worm, not a man." Psalm 22:7
- "Though harshly treated, he submitted and did not open his mouth; Like a lamb led to slaughter or a sheep silent before shearers..." Isaiah 53:7
- "Rejoice with those who rejoice, weep with those who weep." Romans 12

Notes

- "Do whatever he tells you." John 2:5
- "And behold, the veil of the sanctuary was torn in two from top to bottom." Matthew 27:51
- "I would create the universe again just to hear you say that you love me." Jesus to St. Teresa of Avila.

The Defiled Tomb

- "(and you yourself a sword will pierce)" Luke 2:35
- "Behold, I make all things new." Revelation 21:5
- "I am the good shepherd, and I know mine and mine know me." John 10:14
- "...from glory to glory" 2 Corinthians 3:18
- The image of the Sacred Heart revealed to St. Margaret Mary Alacoque

Holy Ground

- "I came so that they might have life and have it more abundantly." John 10:10
- "He is like a tree planted near streams of water, that yields its fruit in season; Its leaves never wither." Psalm 1:3
- "The LORD, your God... will rejoice over you with gladness... will sing joyfully because of you, as on festival days." Zephaniah 3:17-18
- "... the sheep follow him, because they recognize his voice." John 10:4
- "We know that all things work for good for those who love God, who are called according to his purpose." Romans 8:28
- "I have told you this so that my joy may be in you and your joy may be complete." John 15:11
- "The greater the valley, the more glorious the garden." Inspired by *The Butterfly Circus*, short film
- "Life with Christ is a wonderful adventure." Pope St. John Paul II

Back Cover

- "What do you picture when you imagine the landscape of your heart?" inspired by a talk given by Sr. Magnificat Rose, SV

ACKNOWLEDGEMENTS

Cristina Conway, my co-author and friend, thank you for agreeing to this crazy project when I could offer you nothing more than an invitation. Thank you for helping me find my voice.

Rose McShane, thank you for your constant encouragement and "hype of the drip." You have truly championed me in this project and in life. It means more than you know.

Athena Del Aguila, Deanna Chavez, Grace Rivera, and Hannah O'Brien, thank you for loving me in my years of illness and for being witnesses to a God who keeps His Promises.

Alyssa Conway, Calli Carlson, and Lacey Shelley, thank you for walking beside me in the valleys and the gardens of life. I know Jesus more personally having known the three of you.

Genesis Torrens, thank you for listening to my story around the firepit in 2018. You played a pivotal role in my healing and my desire to share my story. Let's have more pizza rolls soon.

MH, thank you for helping to unburden me. Donna Rodgers, thank you for not falling asleep.

Joyce Coronel, thank you for editing this book for us. Thank you for exemplifying so beautifully what it means to use your gift of writing for Jesus, and thank you for helping me do the same.

Hosanna Wong, thank you for seeing the value in my story and for your encouragement in this project. Thank you for sharing your time and gifts to help us get this book into peoples' hands.

Mike Fontecchio, thank you for sharing your publishing expertise and creative insights to bring this project across the finish line. Your gift for design enhances every word in this book.

To all who have accompanied me, encouraged me, and listened to my story, thank you. And finally, to those who are chronically ill, you are loved and your story isn't over.

ABOUT THE AUTHORS

Catherine Mulhern is a storyteller from Arizona. Once chronically ill, she now lives an abundant life which many have called "miraculous." Her gift for writing about the grief and grit of life draws readers more deeply into the beauty, messiness, and glory of the human experience.

Cristina Conway is a teacher and writer living in Arizona. Her passion for the art of literature began 12 years ago when she started creating her own stories, and she was featured in a collection of short stories published at Grand Canyon University. She is enthusiastic about bringing stories to life, whether with her students or anyone willing to hear.

Catherine and Cristina would love to connect with you!

@A.NEW.GARDEN